"So You'll Have Dinner With Me?" Buck Persisted.

"Not unless you tell me why you're here." Cory made her voice sound as firm as she could.

"Mull it over. I think you'll change your mind."

"And why is that?"

"Natural curiosity." He grinned and leaned a little closer to her.

"You seem to have forgotten that I don't like to be toyed with, Buck." She had to fight to keep from being drawn by the spell of those arresting brown eyes. He had no right to look so attractive.

"You should want to go out to dinner with me for old times' sake," he replied. "We've known each other since we were ten."

"Correction," she said. "We knew each other *when* we were ten, and then we met once a year until we were twenty. That was it."

"Really?" His deep voice had sunk almost to a whisper. "There was a little more to it than that, as I recall."

GW00418010

Dear Reader:

Welcome! You hold in your hand a Silhouette Desire – your ticket to a whole new world of reading pleasure.

As you might know, we are continuing the *Man of the Month* concept through to May 1991. In the upcoming year look for special men created by some of our most popular authors: Elizabeth Lowell, Annette Broadrick, Diana Palmer, Nancy Martin and Ann Major. We're sure you will find these intrepid males absolutely irresistible!

But Desire is more than the *Man of the Month*. Each and every book is a wonderful love story in which the emotional and sensual go hand-in-hand. A Silhouette Desire can be humorous or serious, but it will always be satisfying.

For more details please write to:

Jane Nicholls
Silhouette Books
PO Box 236
Thornton Road
Croydon
Surrey
CR9 3RU

CATHRYN CLARE

FIVE BY TEN

Silhouette Desire

Originally Published by Silhouette Books
a division of
Harlequin Enterprises Ltd.

First published in Great Britain in 1991 by Silhouette Books, Eton House, 18-24 Paradise Road, Richmond, Surrey TW9 1SR

© Cathy Stanton 1990

Silhouette, Silhouette Desire and Colophon are Trade Marks of Harlequin Enterprises B.V.

ISBN 0 373 58076 2

22 – 9102

Made and printed in Great Britain

CATHRYN CLARE

is a transplanted Canadian who moved south of the border after marrying a far-from-proper Bostonian. She and her husband now live in an old house in central Massachusetts, where she divides her time between writing and renovation. "Three cats and a view of the forest outside my office window help with the writing part," she says.

Other Silhouette Books by Cathryn Clare

Silhouette Desire

To the Highest Bidder
Blind Justice
Lock, Stock and Barrel

Prologue

The theme music was jaunty, upbeat. It signaled the end of the episode, as the camera panned across the hopeful young faces. There were five of them, twenty years old and ready to take on the world. The actor, relating some anecdote with theatrical skill, was, as usual, the center of attention. The dancer was laughing, her head thrown back in enjoyment. Even the scholar was letting himself go for a change, grinning at the actor's exaggerations.

By comparison, the two at the end of the table were serious. Over the course of ten years of the show, the young woman with the shoulder-length dark blond hair had always shown a formal sort of charm, no doubt suited to her chosen career as a chef and restaurateur. It wasn't unusual for her to sit quietly, almost privately, while the others cavorted for the cameras.

It *was* unusual for the man next to her to be so withdrawn. With the powerful build of an athlete and the prospect of a professional sports career just ahead of him, he somehow seemed older than the others. And until this final shot, he'd always been rowdier, as well. Now he sat, his dark eyes unreadable, deep in thought.

The credits rolled as the actor finished his story. *Five by Ten*. The letters passed by the young faces. Produced and Directed by Theodore Aiken.

Behind the credits, the close-up shots of the faces continued. The young blond woman seemed calm, but something in her eyes suggested she was struggling to appear that way. In the second before the camera moved on, she turned her head slightly, casting a glance in the direction of the dark-eyed athlete next to her. It was a split-second movement, half-lost behind the listing of technicians' names rolling across the screen, and probably not one of the millions of viewers even caught it. But in that subtle gesture and in the sudden widening of her lovely eyes, there was a powerful anguish.

The camera moved on to the face of the man next to her, but not in time to catch his response to whatever her glance had meant. A slight tightening of his jaw muscles was the only movement he made, although his eyes looked almost angry when he raised them briefly to the camera's level.

Through ten years of the *Five by Ten* series, the director had always stressed one thing: the sense of hope embodied in these five talented young people. But for these two, at least, something had cast a shadow over the bright futures that stretched ahead of them. The music was as breezy as ever as the show concluded, but a keen observer would have felt that for this young man and woman, hope was the very furthest thing from their minds.

One

For some reason, Thursday afternoons were always slow at the dentist's office. Maybe people used up all their resolve early in the week, Cory thought, or maybe by Thursday they were looking forward to the weekend and didn't want to spoil things with new fillings or sore gums.

Whatever the reason, she always seemed to have time on her hands on Thursday afternoons. She'd already gotten caught up on her filing and had cleaned the reception area, and there weren't many calls to keep her busy at the phone. With a glance around the nearly empty waiting room, Cory pulled the latest food magazine issue out of her purse and started flipping through it.

I must be some sort of a masochist, she thought, turning the glossy pages. The chicken breasts with lime and chive butter looked tasty. She'd created a similar dish once, using tarragon instead of chives. There was an article on wine cellars, and she couldn't help but think of the cases and cases of wine she still had in her own cellar, salvaged from the Horn of Plenty. Somehow, she could never bring herself to drink any of it.

She flipped another page and stopped. There was a spread on one of the awards dinners that restaurant people staged so many of. The photo spread showed men in tuxes and women in a wild assortment of fancy clothes, with the beaming winners of this year's awards prominently featured. Among them was the young man who'd won this year's Innovative Young Chef prize, and Cory's eyes were irresistibly drawn to the picture. *Four years ago that was me,* she thought glumly and closed the magazine. She wasn't *that* much of a masochist.

The phone rang, startling her out of her thoughts. "Dr. Leary's office," she said into the receiver, sounding as upbeat and efficient as she could.

Evidently she didn't do a very good job of it. "You sound like you just lost your last friend," said a familiar voice.

"Thanks, Annie." Cory leaned her chin on her free hand. "I've just been looking at a cooking magazine."

"Oh, God. Not again."

"I don't know why I do it, to be honest with you."

"Neither do I," said Annie. "It's like someone who's broke and cold in New England spending their time looking at brochures for Caribbean vacations, I guess. You hope it'll help, but it really just makes you feel worse."

"You have quite a way with words," Cory said, laughing now.

"I should, considering what I get paid for them." Annie was a lawyer, and their standing joke was that all of their conversations during working hours were billed at Annie's professional rates. In actual fact, she was also a friend and had been a valued customer at Horn of Plenty before Cory had had to close the restaurant. The bills for handling Cory's rather complicated legal affairs since then had always been ridiculously low.

"Well, if the meter's running, then let's get to business," Cory said. "What's up?"

"Well, I've had a phone call from someone named Theodore Aiken." Cory didn't answer right away, and Annie went on. "Wasn't he the director of those shows you were on as a kid?"

Cory finally found her voice. "Yes," she said, "but those were done with ten years ago. Why is he calling me now?"

"Well, he wouldn't tell me. Apparently he wants to talk to you personally. He left a number for you to call."

Cory was frowning now, tapping her pen against the side of her typewriter. "Why did he call you, I wonder, and not me?"

"He said he didn't have a current number for you. He tried the chamber of commerce to find out why there was no listing for your restaurant anymore, and they put him on to me. You remember that's what we arranged, when all those journalists kept calling up two years ago."

"I remember." Cory's mouth was set in a slightly grim smile.

"Anyway, I wouldn't give him your number, because I didn't know if you wanted to talk to him. But I said I would pass on the message, so that's what I'm doing."

"I see. Thanks, Annie." Cory scribbled down the number Annie gave her, and added, "Be sure to send me a bill."

"Oh, I will." There was an uncharacteristic note of curiosity in Annie's voice as she said, "You know, you've never said much about that show, Cory."

Cory went back to tapping her pen against the typewriter. "There's not much to tell," she said evasively.

"Oh, come on, Cory. Ten years' worth of a nationally televised show, directed by one of the biggest names in the television industry? It must have been quite an experience."

"That's a very good way to put it," Cory said, fighting against the flood of memories that still, after ten years, had the power to swamp her. "It was quite an experience."

"Going all silent on me, huh? Well, all right. But just let me know what Aiken wants, will you? Maybe he's thinking of doing a new show about lady attorneys in their forties. It could be my big break."

"With Theodore, anything's possible," Cory said, smiling now. "One thing's certain. He's *not* going to be interested in following the careers of ex-chefs now working as secretaries."

"You never know."

The two had their usual conversation about when they could get together for lunch—Annie's busy schedule made setting a date nearly impossible—and then they hung up. Cory sighed as she put down the telephone. Only two years ago, she'd been a busy career woman, too.

She stuffed the cooking magazine back in her purse and decided that this was as good a time as any to tackle the dreaded typing file. Her job didn't require much typing, for which she was profoundly grateful. But every now and then the little typing projects would mount up, and she would hunt and peck her way through them. It was hard, at times like these, not to contrast her slowness at the typewriter with her lightninglike speed at whipping together an omelet or devising a menu for a four-course meal.

Putting thoughts of menus and omelets firmly out of her head, she started the first sheet, a finicky retyping of Dr. Leary's rate schedule. She was halfway through it—and a new bottle of correction fluid—when the phone rang.

"Dr. Leary's office," she said, picking it up, grateful for the interruption.

"Is this Cory Vandergill?"

The man's voice was deep and full, and somehow familiar.

"Yes," she replied.

"Will you be there until five o'clock?"

It was almost a demand, as though the question were important.

"Yes," she acknowledged again. His voice stirred some very uncomfortable echoes, but she told herself it was only because she'd been thinking of Theodore that this unidentified voice reminded her of Buck. And then the stranger hung up, leaving Cory looking foolishly at the receiver.

"Who *was* that masked man?" she asked herself out loud, and saw the single waiting patient give her a curious look. She went back to her typing, puzzling over the phone call but not getting anywhere with it.

Until half an hour later, when the reception room door opened and Buck Daly walked in.

She might not have been sure about his voice, but she would have known the man himself in a crowd of a thousand people. It wasn't just the athletic, six-foot-plus frame or that easy, self-confident walk, almost a swagger, that had made him a pinup for teenagers of both sexes—the boys had idolized him for his hockey prowess, while their sisters dreamed about his dark-haired good looks. It was that look in his brown eyes, the look that said *I make myself at home wherever I happen to be*.

Cory remembered the look. He'd managed to make himself at home in her heart once, years ago. He was looking around the small waiting room now with that same proprietary expression, and it put her immediately on her guard.

"Well, well," she said. "I thought I recognized that voice on the phone."

He was wearing a dark green down jacket, protection against the bitter, New Hampshire January outside. It made his brown eyes seem even darker, especially when he came and leaned his arms on the receptionist's counter at disturbingly close range.

"Sorry I hung up without introducing myself," he said. His smile was as engaging as ever. "I had a sneaking feeling I might not be entirely welcome."

"So you decided to drop by in person, where I couldn't hang up on you."

"Something like that."

She wished he'd stop smiling at her. He was entirely too attractive when he smiled. His thick brown hair was cut shorter than it had been ten years ago, but she still remembered the feel of it between her fingers, and the sensation of knowing that seductive smile was meant just for her.

She also remembered her conversation with Annie a few minutes ago. "This must be reunion time," she said, leaning back in her padded chair. "I just got a message that Theodore was looking for me, too."

His smile never wavered. It brought out a hidden dimple in one cheek, just as it always had since he was a small boy. "As a matter of fact, he and I are on the same errand," he said.

"And what is that?"

Buck glanced over his shoulder at the older woman sitting patiently in the waiting room. "Could we go somewhere where we can talk a little more . . . privately?"

"I told you, I work until five."

"Have dinner with me, then. After work."

God help her, she was feeling weak in the knees just looking at him. She couldn't believe he still had this powerful an effect on her, especially when he'd caused her such pain.

They'd caused each other pain, she reminded herself, and knew that was part of why she was so shaky now. There was a look in his dark brown eyes that brought back memories of his own hurt, as well as her own.

That still didn't mean she was going to let him call the shots. There was a mystery here, and she wasn't taking another step until it was cleared up.

"First tell me why you're here, and what Theodore was calling about," she said. "Then maybe I'll think about going out to dinner with you."

"It's sort of complicated. I'd rather wait until I have your undivided attention."

He had it now, but she wasn't going to let him know just how riveting she found his good looks and engaging smile. "Thursdays are always slow around here," she said instead. "Can't you put it in twenty-five words or less, and get it over with?"

"Definitely not. Anyway, I was looking forward to taking you to dinner. You always know the best places to eat."

Darn you, Buck Daly, she wanted to say. Having him here was like having her own past come back to mock her. She looked closely at him, trying to figure out whether he knew about the circumstances of her change in career. His handsome face looked guileless at the moment. Unfortunately, he seemed to be taking her scrutiny for the acceptance he wanted.

"So you'll come?" he persisted.

"Not unless you tell me why you're here." Cory made her voice as firm as she knew how.

Buck sighed good-naturedly. "Well, I don't mind giving you time to think it over," he said. "I think you'll change your mind."

"And why is that?"

"Natural curiosity." He grinned at her, leaning a little farther over the counter.

"You seem to have forgotten that I don't like to be toyed with, Buck."

"Cory, I drove for five hours to get here from New York City. Won't you even give me a couple of hours of your time?"

Cory had to fight to keep herself form being drawn under the spell of those arresting brown eyes. He had no right to look so boyish. He was exactly the same age she was, and these days she felt pretty darned old and jaded.

"You should want to go out to dinner with me for old times' sake," he added. "We've known each other since we were ten, for crying out loud."

She didn't like the arrogance of his demand. You should want to go out to dinner with me, indeed!

"Correction, Mr. Daly," she said crisply. "We knew each other *when* we were ten. And then we met once a year until we were twenty. That was it."

"Really?" His deep voice had sunk almost to a whisper, so that only Cory could hear it. "There was a little more to it than that, as I recall it."

Her hands were shaking now in earnest, and she tried to tell herself it was anger making her feel this way. Buck had no right to march into her life like this and disrupt it with a couple of well-chosen remarks.

"That still doesn't obligate me to have dinner with you," she said, not quite as firmly as she'd planned to.

"Well," he said philosophically, "I don't have anything planned for the rest of the afternoon. And it's a lot warmer in here than it is outside. Mind if I have a seat?"

He sat down without waiting for her answer, and Cory decided that her best defense was just to pretend he wasn't there. She turned back to her half-typed list, annoyed to find that her fingers were less cooperative than ever. She tried to keep her mind on the rows of figures, but Buck Daly's presence kept interfering with her concentration.

It was hard enough to work while he was just sitting there silently. When he began to chat with the other woman in the waiting room, Cory couldn't help but listen in.

"You know, you look sort of familiar," the woman said. "Do I know you from somewhere?"

Cory waited for the inevitable explanation that Buck was the star center for the Chicago Blackhawks. Or did he play for some other team now? She'd stopped keeping track of hockey some time ago.

To her surprise, Buck didn't mention his NHL career. "Well, you might have seen a television show I was on," he said. "It was called *Five by Ten*."

"I don't think so," the woman said doubtfully, looking hard at Buck's handsome face.

"It ran once a year for ten years," he explained. "This director in New York, Theodore Aiken, had an idea that it would be interesting to take a group of kids and follow them from when they were ten till they were twenty."

"You look older than twenty," the woman said doubtfully.

"Well, the show stopped ten years ago."

"And you're one of the kids it featured?"

"Yes," he replied. "And so's Miss Vandergill—the receptionist." He nodded casually toward Cory's desk. "She's the New Englander, and I'm the token Midwesterner. There are three others—one from Louisiana, one from California, and one from Colorado. We were all born in January of 1960."

"How interesting. So you all have birthdays this month."

"Yep. I've already gotten the dreaded event over with. Miss Vandergill's birthday is...this weekend, isn't it, Cory?" He raised his voice slightly.

"Sunday," she murmured, typing fiercely.

"It would be interesting to see what's happened to everyone in ten years," the woman said, almost as if she'd been coached.

"It would, wouldn't it? We all had some pretty grandiose dreams, I can tell you." Buck's voice had become "just-folks," Cory noted. It was as though he'd dropped in to chat with a neighbor, instead of having driven five hours from New York for some reason he wouldn't divulge.

"Have any of those dreams come true?" The woman patient was really getting into the spirit of the thing, no doubt charmed by Buck's potent personality.

"Well, mine sure didn't. And there was one girl who was going to be a Broadway star who's now a housewife. I don't know about the other two. And I'm not sure about Miss Vandergill, either. But I'll bet you it would make good television, to track down all five of us again and do another show."

Cory almost heard the click in her brain. "Oh, no, Buck," she said quickly. "You've got to be kidding."

"You don't think it's a good idea?" He looked up at her again.

"I take it that's not just a hypothetical question," she shot back.

There it was again, that boyish smile she'd fallen so hard for as a teenager. He looked utterly relaxed, his down jacket unbuttoned and his long legs stretched out in front of him. The strength of his thighs was apparent in the way his muscles showed tightly against his jeans, and when he raised his arms to clasp his hands behind his head, she could sense the matching strength of his upper body.

Well, of course, Cory told herself sensibly. The man is a world-class athlete. That magnificent body is just a tool of his trade, the way whisks and sauté pans had once been tools of hers. Of course, she'd never caught herself fantasizing about kitchen gadgets the way she often had about Buck's long, hard body.

"As a matter of fact, it isn't," he said. "Care to hear the rest of the details over dinner tonight?"

He looked very cocky, as though he were sure he had her hooked now. He couldn't possibly know how the thought of another *Five by Ten* affected her, Cory thought miserably. She remembered the barrage of publicity that had surrounded the closing of her restaurant, and cringed inside at the idea of going on national television and spreading the news of her failure to millions of viewers.

"No thank you," she said firmly, and saw the surprise on his face. She'd been right, she thought: he'd been certain she would say yes.

"Why not?" he demanded.

"That's my own business." She went back to typing.

"But Miss Vandergill—" the waiting patient came to Buck's aid "—I'm sure people would love to know what's happened to all five of you."

"And *I'm* sure people have forgotten all about the show," she replied, trying to stay calm. Trust Buck to find himself an ally, she thought.

"That's not true, as a matter of fact." He was on his feet again, leaning over her counter. "Theodore's been getting lots of mail from people wondering why there's never been a follow-up. Sequels are hot right now, you know."

"Maybe for disaster movies," Cory said. She could see the woman getting to her feet now, too, and she had the distinct impression that she was being ganged up on.

She took a deep breath. She'd encountered lots of sticky situations in her restaurant career, and she'd been famous for her tact in dealing with unreasonable patrons and unreliable suppliers. Surely she could call on some of that tact now to get Buck Daly off her case.

The problem was, all she wanted to do was pick him up and toss him out of the office. It was maddening enough to have him here, but to have him enlisting strangers on his side against her—

The intercom on her desk buzzed. "Would you please send Mrs. Rollings in now, Cory?" Dr. Leary asked, and Cory stood up with a distinct feeling of having had her prayers answered for once.

"Dr. Leary will see you now," she said. "In the second room down the hall."

The patient gave her a frankly curious stare on the way, and it took all Cory's goodwill to keep from wishing that the dentist would find at least one cavity. Then she reminded herself that it wasn't Mrs. Rollings she was mad at. It was Buck Daly, and she still hadn't decided what to do about him.

"Nice try," she commented, sitting back down to her typing. "I suppose it would have been too simple, when that woman said you looked familiar, just to tell her you're a big hockey star."

An odd look crossed his face, a kind of amused resignation. "I thought she might have seen *Five by Ten*" he said offhandedly. "Lots of people did, you know—it was a very popular show."

"I'm glad you said 'was,'" she returned.

"And lots of people are looking forward to seeing more of it," he said.

"They'll just have to be disappointed, then. I'm not having my life turned into a peep show for the whole country."

"You didn't seem to mind that ten years ago."

"Things have changed since then."

"Care to tell me how?"

He clearly wasn't going to give up, Cory thought. But every look at his determined, self-confident face made her more certain she'd made the right choice. She'd been hurt badly enough by the local publicity she'd gotten in the past couple of years. Nationwide coverage of the Horn of Plenty scandal would be just too hard to take.

"No," she said bluntly. "And it doesn't matter how many times you ask me—that's all the answer you're going to get. Now I've got a lot to do here, Buck, so if you don't mind . . ."

She let the sentence trail off, hoping desperately that he'd take the hint. He didn't.

"You don't look very busy to me," he commented. "No customers waiting, no phones ringing."

"That just means I have to catch up on paperwork."

She wished she could come up with a seventy-words-per-minute blaze of typing, just to make some sound in the quiet office. But when she went back to her typewriter, the sparse tap-tapping at the machine she'd never quite mastered only seemed to make the silence louder.

Buck let the silence last for several minutes, as though he were considering his next move. Finally he said, "You know, I had quite a time tracking you down."

She'd been so astonished at the sight of him that she hadn't wondered how he *had* managed to track her down. Her phone number was unlisted, and two years ago she'd taken to having her mail delivered to a post office box. It had been too upsetting to have anonymous letters accusing her of being a poisoner coming to her house.

"How did you find me, just out of interest?" she asked Buck.

He smiled at her, as if relieved to find out she still showed *some* curiosity about his visit. "I got in touch with Arlene," he said, naming the dancer who'd been one of the participants on *Five by Ten*.

"I didn't think she had my work phone number."

"She doesn't. In fact, she said you'd become pretty darn reclusive in the past couple of years. But she did say you'd written one Christmas to tell her you were working in a dentist's office. I figured, how many dentists can there be in a place like Keene?" He smiled, and she noticed that the lines around his eyes made him look older than his thirty years. The boyishness of his grin had kept her from noticing it before now.

"There are quite a few," she told him, smiling back in spite of herself.

"*Now* you tell me. I just started working my way through the phone book, calling all of them, until I found you."

"How long did that take?" It was a bit of a shock to remember his pit-bull-like persistence.

He shrugged. "A couple of hours. I found you about three-quarters of the way through the list." He cleared his throat, as though he wasn't sure how to phrase his next remark. "To be honest, Cory, I was pretty surprised when Arlene told me you were a secretary now."

Cory bristled, preparing to defend her privacy. "Why were you surprised?" she asked.

"Well, I figured I'd come up here and find you running some fancy little restaurant. I had my mouth all set for one of your meals, as a matter of fact."

"There are lots of nice little places in Keene," she said coolly. "If you're looking for dinner, I can recommend some of them to you."

She was sure he wouldn't let her get away with a casual change of subject like that. She stabbed a couple of keys viciously and made another in a long series of errors. Sighing, she picked up the bottle of correction fluid.

"So why *aren't* you running a restaurant?" he asked.

She was annoyed at the way her fingers were shaking. "Damn," she said, as though she hadn't heard his question. "I hate these little brushes. Why don't they make this stuff in spray cans?"

"Cory?"

She looked reluctantly over the counter and saw that although he'd returned to his seat in the waiting room, he'd abandoned his earlier relaxed pose. He was leaning forward now, elbows on his knees, and the look he was giving her seemed calculated to look into her very soul.

She gave up evading the question. "I *was* running a restaurant, for a while," she admitted.

"Why aren't you running it now?"

"It closed."

He must have heard the tightness in her voice and the pain behind her words. He looked puzzled and mercifully, let the question drop. His smile faded, and those little lines around his eyes deepened. Somewhere in the past ten years, he looked as though he'd learned some difficult lessons, just as she had.

He was silent for what seemed like a long while, and once again Cory struggled to keep her attention on the rate sheet. Tap. Tap. Her own inefficient typing sounded ridiculous to her ears.

And presumably to Buck's, too. After she'd tapped and cursed and corrected her way almost to the end of the page, he asked, "How many words a minute do you type?"

Her head whipped up as she glared at him. "These aren't words," she informed him. "They're numbers. They take longer."

"I see."

She hated the amusement in his voice. And worse yet was the hint that he knew she wasn't a real secretary, just a refugee from the food service industry. If he needled her long enough, his tone seemed to say, he was sure she'd break down and tell him how she'd gotten there.

Well, she wasn't about to do that. "The typing isn't a very big part of this job," she said defensively. "Dr. Leary wanted somebody who could be pleasant at dealing with the public."

"Like you're dealing with me?"

"You're not the public. If you want to come in here to get a tooth capped, I'll be as pleasant as you like."

He smiled, and she could see the flash of his even white teeth. "No, thanks," he said. "I've had enough encounters with dentists to last me a lifetime. Occupational hazard."

They must have been skillful dentists, Cory thought. If Buck had lost some of his teeth, as almost every hockey player did, it certainly wasn't obvious.

"Are you on vacation or something?" she asked, suddenly wondering how an NHL star could find time off in the middle of January.

"Something like that." There it was again, that mix of amusement and resignation. "Look, Cory, I'm going to need a place to stay for the next few days. Can you recommend a good hotel nearby?"

"How many days?" She could hear the wariness in her own voice.

He seemed to hear it, too, and she could tell it pleased him. Had he just been waiting for her to show an interest in him?

When he didn't answer, she went on. "Depends on what you're here for. There hasn't been much snow this winter, but if you want skiing, there are a couple of good places. Or if you're into country inns, I can tell you about several of those. Or if you want to be in bustling downtown Keene—"

He didn't let her finish. As smoothly as a big cat, he stood up and moved over to her desk. Once again she felt that he was too close, standing there with his forearms on the counter.

"I'm here to see you," he said bluntly.

She couldn't think of a bright reply to that one. For half an instant it was very tempting to lose herself in the smoldering closeness of those dark brown eyes.

Then she shook herself back into some kind of common sense. He *was* here to see her, of course—to see if he could talk her into doing another segment of *Five by Ten*. And from the look on his face, it meant a lot more to him than just an hour's worth of entertainment for the viewing public.

"Why are you so set on having this show taped?" she asked him. To her infinite satisfaction, it was his turn to look evasive.

"I have my reasons," he said.

"Such as?"

"If you have dinner with me tonight, I'll tell you."

She should just continue to say no, she thought. It was her best line of defense. But her curiosity—and something more—had definitely been sparked.

"I'm warning you right now that nothing you can say will change my mind," she said.

"That's fine."

She remembered the way he would seize hold of a project and work at it until he'd gotten what he wanted. Was this his newest project? Or was there more to it than that? Cory closed her eyes briefly, wishing she could quell the feelings that were rising inside her. Buck's all-consuming drive to succeed had come between them so devastatingly ten years ago, and she doubted if she had the strength to deal with his obsessiveness again.

"Do you have a car?" she asked, opening her eyes abruptly.

"Yes. Why don't you recommend one of those hotels, and I can go and check in while you finish work? I'll pick you up at five."

"Make it six. You can pick me up at home after I get changed."

She told him about a couple of the most likely hotels nearby, then gave him her address. "It's the top buzzer," she said. "There's no name next to the button."

He raised his eyebrows in a silent question, but once again she didn't bother explaining about her cherished anonymity. When he'd finally closed the door of the waiting room behind him, she was amazed at the combination of relief and regret she felt. His effect on her was more unsettling than ever. She could still hear his velvet-smooth voice, and feel her stepped-up heartbeat, caused by the look in his dark eyes.

She made herself take a deep breath to calm down. It was just after four, and she decided she had a shot at clearing out the rest of the typing file, if she got back to work right away and hunted and pecked diligently until five. First, though, she picked up the phone and made one quick call.

She wasn't a hockey fan herself and had purposely ignored the game after her painful breakup with Buck ten years ago. Annie, on the other hand, was a dedicated follower. Cory dialed her lawyer's number, hoping Annie would be too busy to comment on her friend's sudden interest in a sport she'd always avoided.

"Just a quick trivia question, Annie," she said, when she got through. "I need to know about a hockey player named Buck Daly."

"Buck Daly." Annie took a thoughtful pause. "Star defenseman for the Blackhawks. Rookie of the year several years ago."

Ten years, Cory added mentally, but didn't say anything.

"Broke a couple of records in his rookie year, and a couple since then, I believe."

"What about now?" Cory asked. "Does he still play?"

"No, not since the '87 season. He broke his ankle in too many places to fix it, as I recall. He's been retired since then. I don't know what he's doing now."

Neither do I, Cory thought, as she thanked Annie and hung up the phone. *But I have a feeling I'm about to find out.*

Two

___

Buck was feeling half-hypnotized by the snowflakes settling on his windshield. The weatherman had predicted only a light dusting of snow, but already the frozen ground was covered in white, and the big flakes were drifting down just quickly enough that they kept catching his eye.

He was still a few minutes early. He didn't want to ring Cory's doorbell before six, but he was finding it hard to wait patiently. He was amazed at his eagerness to see her again. And every time he closed his eyes and pictured her the way she'd looked this afternoon, that eagerness grew a little more and threatened to turn into something much like need.

She was as graceful and willowy as he remembered, and her sandy blond hair was as satin smooth and shiny. She'd worn it loose today, like a glossy curtain that just touched her shoulders. The last time he'd seen her it had been twisted into a stylish braid that accented her high cheek-bones and the elegant lines of her small, determined chin.

He'd always thought whimsically that she was like a princess out of a fairy tale, and even seeing her in the setting of a dentist's office hadn't dispelled that impression. There was a faraway look in those wide blue-green eyes that made her seem somehow removed from humdrum, every-day life.

Damn it all, he thought, clenching a fist against the steering wheel. He'd come up here thinking that Theodore's proposed new show would be a good opportunity to see Cory again and put to rest the ghost that had been haunting him for ten years. Instead, the ghost turned out to be flesh and blood and just as alluring as ever. The instant he'd seen her today, he'd recalled every second of their last and most painful encounter.

Well, it wasn't in Buck's nature to dwell on past failures. He glanced at his watch. It was just before six, and his impatience was getting the better of him. Still picturing Cory's sea-green eyes and full, soft lips, he opened his car door and stepped out into the snowy evening.

Cory had decided that she wasn't going to let Buck Daly fluster her. She'd found herself rushing to get home from work, and dithering seriously about what to wear to dinner. She wasn't usually a ditherer, and when she'd hauled the third outfit out of her closet only to reject it, she made herself stop and take a deep breath.

"He is a very attractive man," she admitted out loud, "and he's stirring up some memories. *And* he's here about something that I'm sensitive about. But that's still no reason to be acting like a fifteen-year-old."

Over the years Cory had considered getting a cat, so that there would be someone to listen when she talked to herself. It was a habit she couldn't seem to break. And as always, it helped. Once she'd given herself that stern little talking-to, she could get on with the business of getting ready. She donned a simple wool jersey dress in an aquamarine color that matched her eyes, and a silver and turquoise belt, then put her hair up in a twist behind her head and secured it with a silver clasp. Finally she felt calm enough to meet a whole team of all-stars.

That didn't quite keep her heart rate from accelerating when the doorbell rang. When she met Buck on the doorstep and found herself once again so close to those watchful brown eyes and handsome, strongly chiseled features, she was perilously close to feeling like an infatuated fifteen-year-old again.

"Looks like the weatherman lied," she said, peering out into the thickening snow outside.

"Give the guy a break," Buck smiled. "Predicting the weather in New England has got to be a thankless job, at best."

He was watching her closely as she put on her navy down coat and gloves. She could feel the warmth of his body in the little vestibule, and his nearness was doing wild things to her pulse. She looked up fleetingly into his eyes and saw a hunger there that matched what she was feeling inside. Quickly, she looked away.

"So, shall we go?" she said brightly, aware of the little quaver in her voice. "I made reservations at a little place—"

He cut her off. "Just a minute," he said. "There's something I meant to tell you this afternoon, but somehow I just didn't get around to it." She felt her eyes widen slightly as he reached for her.

"What's that?"

His hands were on her shoulders now, strong and possessive. She felt herself melting toward him without willing it. This is right, her senses were telling her. This is good.

His voice was nothing but a throaty murmur—a sound she'd never forgotten but honestly never thought she'd hear again. "I'm glad to see you again, Cory," he said, and before she had time to reply or sort out the wild mix of feelings inside, he bent his head and touched her lips very softly with his own.

It was the briefest of kisses, but instantly Cory's mind was overflowing with the taste and scent of him. Something inside her came pulsing back into life. His hands held her close to his chest, and his lips were slightly parted, allowing her to sense the tightly checked hunger inside him.

When he lifted his head, Cory's heart was racing. She could still feel the warmth of his breath caressing her cheek, and then he moved his head farther away. He, too, looked shaken, as though with the smallest provocation he would gladly have abandoned his pretense at being well-mannered, and swept her off her feet right there in the tiny vestibule.

"I'm . . . glad to see you, too, Buck," Cory managed to say. The words were ridiculously inadequate. "It's just too bad it has to be under these circumstances."

"Ah, yes—the show. I was forgetting we still have business to discuss." His voice was smooth again, but she could tell it was costing him an effort.

"You weren't forgetting that I don't intend to change my mind, I hope," she replied. She was glad he'd mentioned the show; for a moment she'd been in danger of letting Buck's attraction take over her good judgment, but now she had herself back on track.

"And I hope *you* weren't forgetting that I won the NHL award for being a pushy son of a gun, two years running," he said, holding the door open for her.

"I didn't know there was an official award for that."

"Well, they don't say so in so many words." The ringing of his boot heels was slightly muffled by the snow on the sidewalk as he led the way to a dark green car at the curb. "Officially, it's the award for the player who scores the most shorthanded goals. But translated, it means being a pushy son of a gun. Which way do I go?"

"Left at the stop sign. I hope you like Italian food."

"Are you kidding? Pizza, spaghetti and meatballs—"

"That's Italian for tourists," she said, trying to keep the smile out of her voice. She'd forgotten what enjoyable company Buck could be. "I'm talking about *real* Italian food—several courses, nothing too heavy, just a nice blend of tastes."

"I should have known a graduate of New York's fanciest cooking school would go for something more than just pizza."

"Oh, I like pizza, too. It's funny—pizza seems to have found a niche in the world of nouvelle cuisine. I saw a menu the other day that had pizza with goat cheese and herbs on it."

Buck made a face. "I'll stick with plain cheese and pepperoni, thanks," he said.

"You always did have a healthy appetite, as I recall."

"But not a fancy one. I hope the menu with the goat cheese pizza wasn't from the restaurant we're going to."

"Don't worry. It wasn't." Cory looked at him, then back through the snow-dotted windshield. He seemed so completely relaxed again, the way he had been this afternoon at the office. She wondered if she'd imagined the tension in him when he'd kissed her. Maybe he'd meant it as nothing more than a friendly gesture, and her own treacherous senses had embroidered it. It was a little scary to realize how much she'd been missing the magic Buck Daly had once brought to her life. ''You need to make a left at that next light,'' she said. ''The restaurant is immediately on your right. It's that little place with the tile roof.''

''Very Italian,'' he commented, turning the car into the parking lot.

''Actually, I believe it started life as a Mexican place.'' She smiled. ''The current owners bought it about a year ago and got rid of the straw hats and pictures of Acapulco Bay.''

''Do you come here a lot?''

''Not really. I don't eat out that much anymore.''

She didn't bother explaining that since her own involvement in the restaurant trade had come to an abrupt halt, she hadn't enjoyed frequenting other people's restaurants as much as she'd once done.

''Been more into home cooking, have you?''

''You might say that.''

''Lots of those homegrown vegetables, I bet.''

Cory winced. Either Buck really hadn't heard anything about the Horn of Plenty, or he was sadistically determined to hurt her. Looking into his warm brown eyes, she couldn't believe he would deliberately do that. But it hurt anyway.

''You have a good memory,'' was all she said, as they left the car and headed into the restaurant.

''Well, it was pretty hard to forget. Not only were you already written up in two New York magazines for your new veggie recipes by the time you were twenty, but I'll never forget visiting you at the cooking school and seeing that crazy garden you'd set up in the airshaft.''

''It wasn't crazy,'' she said, hearing that note of defensiveness creeping in again. She wished she could just enjoy this evening out with a handsome man she'd happened to have been in love with ten years ago. The trouble was, those

ten years seemed to have melted into the air as though
they'd never been. She felt as attracted and as vulnerable as
she had at twenty. "It was a hydroponic garden," she went
on, calming herself with an effort. "Still the best way to get
fresh lettuce in February."

Getting themselves seated and ordering their dinner was
a very welcome distraction, as far as Cory was concerned.
And it gave her time to collect her wits and to try to put the
memory of Buck's kiss out of her thoughts.

As soon as they'd ordered and the waiter had gone, she
leaned back in her chair and said, "So, what are you doing
with yourself now that you're not a hockey player anymore?"

"You heard about that, did you?"

"Just today, as a matter of fact. I have to admit I haven't
been following sports very closely for the past few years."

"Not even to keep up with my brilliant career?"

The waiter returned with a bottle of white wine and when
her glass had been filled, Cory turned the long stem between her fingers speculatively. "You really *did* have a
brilliant career, didn't you?" she said.

He lifted his glass toward her, and she raised hers in reply. "Here's to my brilliant, if short, career," he said. She
wondered if she detected a trace of bitterness in his words.
"I can't complain. I had a better time in seven seasons than
a lot of athletes have in a lifetime. And thirty's old for a
hockey player, anyway."

Cory shook her head, smiling. "I've always wondered
what it must feel like to be over the hill at twenty-five," she
said. "It must have been hard for you, Buck—having to
stop playing, I mean."

"Well, it wasn't a picnic. And the worst part was how
long it took for my ankle to be usable again, even for
walking. I tend to be fairly impatient about stuff like that."

Cory smothered a smile. "I can imagine," she said.

"Are you implying something about me, Miss Vandergill?"

She let the smile out, mirroring the one on his face. "Just that if I looked under 'impatience' in the dictionary, I'd probably find a picture of you," she told him.

"Well, hockey players who sit around waiting for someone to pass them the puck don't set many records," he said. "My impatience has gotten me a lot of places."

"All of them good?" She was suddenly hungry for information about him. For ten years she'd tried to tell herself he didn't exist, because it was easier that way. But now that he was actually sitting across from her, looking handsomer than ever in his dark brown suit and white shirt, she wanted to know everything that had happened to him in the intervening years.

Actually, she already knew one thing that had happened, and she couldn't help adding wickedly, "What about your marriage? Was that a good thing?"

The sudden cloud on his features surprised her. "Sure wasn't," he said laconically. "But that's all water under the bridge."

Cory remembered the splash his divorce from a Hollywood starlet had made, and the way the size of the alimony settlement had been blazoned all over front pages of the supermarket tabloids.

"You were married pretty young, weren't you?" she persisted.

Buck took a sip of his wine. "Twenty-three," he said. "Stayed married a whole year and a half. But I don't want to talk about that, Cory. I want to know about you."

Cory wasn't at all sure she wanted to tell him about her, and fortunately, their first course arrived to delay the moment. The dish she'd recommended, a combination of fresh mozzarella cheese with basil and tomatoes, drizzled with good olive oil, proved to be a perfectly good distraction.

"You're right. This isn't what I think of as Italian food," Buck admitted. "But it's delicious. Where'd they get tomatoes like this is January?"

"They have their own greenhouse," Cory said. "And a lot of heat lamps and grow-lights and things."

"Are you still as much of a gardener as you used to be?"

He was obviously trying to do some tactful prying, and Cory was quick to head him off. "No," she said shortly.

"Why not?"

She shrugged and speared a piece of tomato with her fork. "It's just one of those things I outgrew," she said.

"I hope you haven't outgrown too many of the things I used to like about you." Buck's words caught her off guard, and she set down her fork as she looked across the table at him. His eyes were serious. "What happened to make all these changes in your life, Cory?"

It wasn't going to work, Cory realized. She couldn't keep putting him off with vague negatives all evening. He was too persistent—and too insightful.

"If I give you a perfectly good reason why I won't do Theodore's show, will you stop badgering me about it?" she asked him.

"I wasn't talking about Theodore's show."

"But that's the real reason you're here," she pointed out. "That's why you're asking all these questions. Isn't it?" Her voice faltered slightly over her last words.

"Is it?" A whimsical smile played over his handsome face and then vanished. "I thought it was, myself, until I saw you again this afternoon."

Cory's heart beat a little faster, but she was careful not to let him know it. "If it's not about the show, then why *are* you here?" she asked him. "And don't try to tell me you just happened to be passing through Keene, because I won't believe you."

He was uncharacteristically silent for a long moment, and when he finally answered, she found she was leaning forward a little to hear what he would say. He frowned into his wineglass as he spoke. "I'll admit the show was what prompted me to come here," he said. "I have a pretty good reason for wanting to see it aired, which I'll get to later. But now that I've seen you again…" He let the words trail off, then looked up at her with that dangerous, hungry look in his eyes again. "Cory, what happened between us ten years ago has been tearing me up ever since. I guess I'm wondering if there isn't some way to put it right."

She gave a short, bitter laugh. "How?" she asked. "By writing a happy ending for it?"

"I don't know." He was glaring at his wineglass again. "All I know is, I didn't expect to feel this way again, and now that I do—"

He broke off again and completed his sentence wordlessly, by reaching across the table and covering her hand with his. Cory was amazed all over again at the way she was drawn to him and wanted to be closer even while her common sense told her loudly that there had been some very good reasons why things hadn't worked out between them. The chances were that the very same things would stand between them if they tried to pick up the pieces now.

She was opening her mouth to tell him so, when she heard her name being called across the small restaurant by a voice she knew all too well.

"Cory Vandergill!" Hector James had to make a big splash, no matter where he was, she thought. She wasn't sure whether she resented or was grateful for the interruption.

"Hello, Heck," she said, turning in her chair as the burly businessman and his wife made their way toward Cory and Buck's table. There was a time when she would have greeted him with a smile, but now she kept her face neutral, not unfriendly, but definitely not welcoming, either. Out of the corner of her eye she could see Buck taking in her guarded expression.

"Nice to see you out enjoying yourself, Cory," Heck was saying expansively. He held out a fleshy hand toward Buck. "Heck James," he said. "I'm an old friend of Cory's."

Buck rose, shaking the man's hand. "Buck Daly," he said. "Also an old friend of Cory's." Cory was amused to see that he was matching her tone, staying carefully neutral in the face of Heck's attempts to be buddies.

"Buck Daly... Not the hockey player? Norma, imagine that. This is my wife, Norma," he added, belatedly. "We both used to be big fans of yours, didn't we, honey? Imagine you showing up in our little town. Vacationing, are you?"

Cory saw other diners turning their way, drawn by Heck's overloud voice. Years ago, she'd found the man's eagerness to be in the middle of things an endearing quality, but even then, she'd always wished she could turn down his volume a little.

"More or less." Buck's voice was much softer by contrast, but his next words were pointed nevertheless. "It's nice to be in a quiet place, to enjoy a quiet dinner with a friend."

Even Heck couldn't miss that hint, and Cory smiled to see him backpedaling. "Oh, well, hey, don't let us interrupt you. Just wanted to say hello. Enjoy your dinner, folks." He waved ostentatiously and threaded his way to his own table, his wife a few steps behind him.

"Is that a local custom?" Buck wanted to know as he sat back down. "The wife walking three paces behind, I mean."

Cory's smile widened. "Well, Heck *does* fancy himself a local potentate, so maybe he prefers it that way. Thanks for shutting him down, Buck. Otherwise he'd probably have suggested we all sit together to eat, and I'd rather eat at a greasy spoon than do that."

"Heck James," he said thoughtfully. "Wasn't there a man named Heck James who was going to be one of your principal backers when you opened that restaurant?"

"Actually, he was *the* backer of my restaurant." Cory speared another piece of tomato from her plate, trying to look disinterested.

"Looks like you came to a parting of the ways."

"Not really. Over the years, as the restaurant did well, I was able to buy him out. By the time the restaurant closed, I was the sole owner."

"Then why were you just looking at Heck James as if he was something just slightly more appealing than a cockroach?" Buck wanted to know.

"I didn't realize I was being that obvious about it."

"Oh, you weren't. But you forgot—I know you pretty well, Cory."

Too darned well, she thought. "It's a long story," she said.

"Which I'd be very interested to hear. Why did you close the restaurant, Cory?"

"Maybe I just burned out."

"And maybe I heard differently. According to the food magazines I read, Horn of Plenty and Cory Vandergill were trendsetters up here in New England. You had a real going concern, as I understood it."

"When did you take up reading food magazines?"

He looked embarrassed. "Just trying to broaden myself, that's all," he replied. "And, well, hell, Cory, it was a way to get news about you. You were getting to be a big deal, weren't you? Writing a regular column in one magazine, and showing up at awards ceremonies all over the place. I heard you were publishing a cookbook, too, and planning a video. And then I was out of commission for a couple of years, not paying much attention to anything while I was injured, and when I got back into the swing of things—poof! Cory Vandergill and Horn of Plenty seemed to have vanished. And what I want to know is, what happened?"

Cory sighed. She was going to tell him at least part of it, and the sooner she got it over with, the better, she supposed. "If I tell you the whole story, it'll just ruin my appetite," she said, trying to stay calm. "But I'll give you the gist of it, and that'll explain why I'm not interested in doing another episode of *Five by Ten*. All right?"

"Go on." He wasn't making any promises, she noticed. She took a deep breath and plunged in.

"I'm involved in a lawsuit," she said. "It happened as a result of my attempts to run a restaurant, and it's also the reason I'm no longer in the restaurant business. I lost the early rounds in the courts, and my lawyer is appealing to the state Supreme Court this spring. And I'm afraid there's a very good chance I'm going to lose there, too."

"How much money do you stand to lose?"

She winced inwardly. "Far more than I can realistically pay," she said.

"Maybe you need a better lawyer."

"I have a perfectly good lawyer. What I need is a defense, and I haven't been able to come up with one."

"Why not?"

"Look at this chicken." She gestured to their main course, which the waiter had just set in front of them. "Wouldn't it be a shame to ruin my appetite for it?"

She was trying to make light of things, but Buck's face told her that he saw how deeply uncomfortable she really was.

"I could probably ask around and get the whole story from someone else," he speculated.

"You could do that," she said. "I'm sure you could dig up the story from the local paper or somewhere."

There it was again—that harsh sound in her own voice. She'd worked hard to keep it from surfacing, but somehow Buck Daly's probing made her more defensive than ever.

"But you'd rather I didn't."

"You're right."

"And I'd rather hear it from you, if I'm going to hear it at all."

"In that case, you're not going to get a chance to satisfy your curiosity, I'm afraid."

"Not at the moment, anyway. I can see that."

"Not in the future, either."

"Hmm." The wordless syllable said a multitude of things, all of which made Cory strangely uneasy. Buck seemed to be hinting that he had no intention of leaving her alone for a while yet.

"Well, now maybe you can understand why I don't want to be on national television," she said briskly, hoping they could wrap up this unsettling conversation. "I don't need any more bad publicity."

"*Five by Ten* wouldn't necessarily be bad," he said. "You would get to tell your side of the story."

"I get to do that in court before long," she said. "I'm not hankering for a dress rehearsal."

"What about Heck James?" Buck asked abruptly. "Where does he fit into all this?"

By now Cory's stomach really was in a knot, and she put down her fork, no longer attempting to hide her true feelings about her one-time backer. "Heck James is nothing but a social climber," she said. "He's your buddy when things look good, but if there's nothing in it for him, he's nowhere to be found."

Buck seemed almost amused by her statement. "I get the feeling there's a story behind *that*," he said.

"There is."

"Maybe you could do the show and just leave out the parts you don't want to talk about," he suggested.

Cory shook her head. "That would be like you refusing to talk about your injury and retirement," she said. "It would look a little odd to pick up my life at twenty, when I was going to be the next Julia Child, and then jump to thirty and show me working in a dentist's office to make ends meet."

"I did wonder how you ended up behind a desk." His dark eyes were smiling now.

"It's called 'paying the rent,'" she said.

"Do you like being a secretary?"

Cory decided to be honest. "Not really," she said. "And as I'm sure you observed this afternoon, my typing speed isn't what got me hired. But at least it's a job."

"Why don't you do something else in the food business? Work in another restaurant, for instance?"

"No one's likely to hire me."

"Come on, Cory. You have tons of qualifications."

"I have a very bad reputation, Buck."

"What did you do, poison someone?"

Cory stiffened, then forced herself to relax again. The smile on his face told her he was trying to make a joke, to lighten the mood. She wasn't about to tell him he'd just guessed her secret.

"Something just as bad," she hedged. At least she was sure now, from his face, that Buck really didn't know the whole story. She was relieved to know he wasn't playing games with her, anyway.

For the moment, he seemed to have decided to stop pestering her with questions. The subject of the television show kept surfacing, though, no matter how Cory tried to steer clear of it.

"Did you know Theodore's getting married again?" Buck asked, as they were finishing their salads and considering what to order for dessert.

"Really? Is this number three?"

"Four, believe it or not. I think he enjoys *getting* married a lot more than he likes *being* married."

"That was always what my father thought." Cory's father, Allen Vandergill, had been a television colleague of Theodore's twenty-five years ago in New York. The two men had stayed friends even after Allan had moved to rural New Hampshire in search of a quieter life-style. "It's funny, you know. Of the five of us on the show, only Arlene is married."

"Do you keep in touch with the other three?" Buck asked.

"Oh, we exchange Christmas cards, and Arlene and I write once in a while."

"Does she still dance at all?"

"No. She says it's something you have to do full-time or not at all. And I think she's more relaxed, anyway, being a wife and mother now."

"Richard is still acting part-time, I gather."

Cory smiled, as people tended to do when the flamboyant actor's name came up. "He was doing summer stock the last time I heard from him," she said. "And spending the rest of the year selling real estate."

"Which I bet he's terrific at."

"I bet you're right. Richard could talk anyone into anything, if he set his mind to it."

She let the words hang as she studied Buck's face. Buck had never had Richard Brett's gift of gab, but there was no doubt of the fierceness of his own determination.

"And Dennis, of course, is still an archaeology professor," she went on hurriedly.

"He never wanted to do anything else, did he?" Buck asked.

"No. Just like you and playing hockey."

"And you and running a restaurant."

They looked speculatively at each other, and Cory could almost hear Buck's thoughts. They were bound to echo her own.

"And now I'm not playing hockey anymore," he said slowly. "And you're not running a restaurant." He cleared his throat, as though he were going to continue, but then he seemed to change his mind.

Cory was glad he had. Things were happening too quickly, and she needed a chance to sort out her feelings. She'd thought her love for Buck was something safely buried, and to find that it was in danger of reviving at a single touch of his hand was disconcerting. Plus he was hinting at thoughts of the two of them trying again, and Cory was sure that was a prescription for disaster.

She studied the dessert menu for a moment, then put it aside, decided to say what was really on her mind. "You've asked me a lot of questions," she said, "but you haven't answered very many of mine. How about the big question, Buck. Why is it so important to you that I go along with Theodore's plans for a new *Five by Ten*?"

Buck, too, put his menu down. She sensed a subtle change in his mood, as though he were shifting gears. At first she couldn't think why his expression seemed familiar to her, and then she remembered. She'd seen Buck play hockey a few times, when *Five by Ten* tapings had coincided with one of his games. The look on his face now was the one she'd seen when he was getting ready to go out on the ice, charging himself up to win.

She remembered, too, how all-important his hockey career had been to him, and seeing that absorbed look again in his eyes made her steel herself.

"Fair enough," he said, clasping his hands behind his head. Cory could see the strength of his arms beneath his tailored suit jacket. "Well, I have a new venture, one I'm pretty excited about. You see, when I was trying to put my ankle back together, I talked to a lot of doctors and therapists and a lot of other players who'd had similar problems. And I did a lot of traveling around, trying to find the best people to patch me up. I discovered that there are good people out there, but finding them is not as easy as you'd think."

He went on, becoming more enthusiastic. Only half of Cory's attention was on his story, though. She was following every detail of his struggle to rehabilitate his shattered ankle, but she was also taking in the new animation and drive in him as he warmed up to the subject.

"So I decided that what the sports world really needs is a new kind of sports medicine clinic, not just to deal with injuries themselves but also the psychological problems an injured athlete has—having to take time off from a career, or abandon it altogether, the way I did. Those things cause a lot of stress."

"So you're going to start a clinic like that?"

"Not just one. That's thinking small. No, we're opening a whole chain of clinics, in seven cities to start with."

"Seven?" Cory must have sounded as startled as she felt, because Buck looked sharply over at her. "That seems pretty ambitious, Buck."

"Well, I told you, that's just the way I operate. Now, the way I see it, we'll put clinics in seven major cities, and if things take off the way I hope they will, we'll have the opportunity to sell franchises in a few years. That way, amateur athletes in smaller towns can have the same facilities as professionals do now. Every Sportsfix branch will have at least four kinds of therapists on the staff...."

And he was off again, describing his grandiose plans while Cory sat silent, listening and watching him. His dark eyes sparkled and he gestured with his hands as he outlined the future he envisioned. And, Cory thought, almost glumly, he was just as passionately involved in this new career of his as he'd been in the old one. She might have known her instincts were right: Buck Daly hadn't changed much over the years, and that meant their problems hadn't changed, either. She'd be wise to resist the potent attraction between them and concentrate on ending Buck's visit as soon as possible.

"All this will involve a lot of travel, I presume," she said, when he paused for breath.

"Well, sure. We're going to use my personal experience as a way of selling the clinics, at first, so I'll be a big part of the advertising and so on. And that's where *Five by Ten* comes in."

Cory had almost forgotten about the show. Now, as Buck leaned forward again, closer to her, all of this started to fall into place with a very unpleasant certainty.

"My name was pretty well-known across the country while I was still playing," he went on. "But things change fast in that business, and I wasn't in it long enough to get to be a legend. According to my publicists, what I've got now is a 'name-recognition problem.'"

"And *Five by Ten* is going to solve that problem for you, is that it?"

"To put it bluntly, yes. Look, I'm not trying to sound like a snake-oil salesman here. I'm not thinking of *Five by Ten* as nothing more than a free TV ad. But from my point of view, it's too good a chance to turn down. You remember the part at the end of each show, where we all got to talk about what we wanted to do next in our lives?"

"I remember." Cory recalled only too clearly the glorious dreams she'd talked about at twenty.

"Well, where's the harm in my talking about Sportsfix? It *is* what I'm planning to do next, after all. And it's the biggest publicity opportunity I could possibly have."

"Why don't you just buy advertising time, if that's what you want?"

"Do you have any idea what TV ad time sells for? One thirty-second spot would eat up more than our entire budget for a year."

Cory knew it was true. She also knew that the thought of having her own disasters aired on national television made her skin crawl with imagined embarrassment. "I guess you're right," she said. "*Five by Ten* does seem like a golden opportunity for you. There's only one thing wrong with it."

"Just because you've had a little setback—"

"It's a little more than that," she retorted. "And for all I know, my lawyer may advise me that going on television could hurt my chances of getting a fair trial."

"That's a cheap excuse." His voice was thick with frustration. Oh, how she remembered that sound!

"Do you want dessert?" she asked, not bothering to be subtle about changing the topic.

"No." He made no move to pick up his menu again.

"Neither do I. Maybe we should be on our way."

They had to pass Heck James's table on their way out, and Cory hoped they could do it unnoticed. But she might have known the opportunistic Heck would never miss a chance to converse with a celebrity. As Buck neared his table, Heck leaned back and said in a whisper that the whole room could hear, "What do you think about the Blackhawks' chances this year, Buck?"

Cory could hear Buck sigh, but he replied civilly enough, "Not much, I'm afraid. Without better goaltending, they're not going to do much."

"That's what I thought myself." Heck seemed to take this agreement on this subject as an opening for further conversation. "Look, while you're in the area, maybe you'd like to come out to our place for a drink some evening. We have a little spread just north of town."

Heck's little spread was half the size of Keene itself, Cory knew. She might be mad at Buck, but that didn't mean she was going to let him fall into the hands of her social-climbing former patron.

"Buck won't be staying long, Heck," she intervened. "He's just passing through, aren't you, Buck?"

She took his arm, not waiting for him to confirm it, and together they headed for the door.

Three

────────

Outside, the snow had proved the weatherman dead wrong. It was piling up at a great rate, and Buck had to clear the car's windows before they could pull out of the parking lot.

"Very picturesque," he muttered as he started the engine. "What's the matter, Cory? You don't look as though you're enjoying it."

She looked cold, he thought, although the efficient heater had already warmed up the inside of the vehicle. Cory was sitting with her arms tightly crossed in front of her, looking anxiously at the road ahead of them.

"Just a little phobia of mine," she said, trying to speak lightly. "I'm not crazy about winter driving, that's all."

"And you call yourself a New Englander."

This attempt at a bantering conversation just wasn't going to work, Buck knew. There were too many serious things still unsaid between them. He carefully negotiated a slippery corner, and then said, "What did you mean by that crack about me not being in the neighborhood for long? I had the feeling you weren't just trying to put Heck James off."

"Not entirely, no." She was still looking nervously through the windshield. "If I promise you that I'll think about doing Theodore's show, will you leave?"

Buck gritted his teeth. "I don't know that you *are* going to do the show," he replied. "And I'm not going anywhere until I hear you say yes."

"Of all the stubborn—" The rest of her words were cut off by a sharp gasp as Buck rounded another corner and the car skidded slightly on the slick pavement. "Buck, aren't you driving a little too fast?"

"It's all right. I'm an old pro at this." Somehow, his words didn't seem to reassure her. He could see her gloved fingers clutching her elbows tightly, and her foot seemed to keep stomping on an invisible brake pedal. "I thought you'd be used to snowstorms, living up here," he commented.

Again she tried for a laugh and almost made it. "I know," she said. "It's irrational, I guess. But my mother was killed when her car skidded off the road in a snowstorm. I guess I've never quite gotten over it."

Buck slowed down a little. "I should have remembered that," he said. "I'm sorry."

"That's okay. No need for you to recall every little detail about me."

They were rounding the last corner onto Cory's street now, and Buck gave Cory a sidelong look. She seemed almost brittle, and he was willing to bet it wasn't all because of the snow. Something had happened during dinner to harden her, and he couldn't quite put his finger on the moment when it had happened.

"You'd be surprised how much I remember about you," he said quietly, pulling into a parking space in front of Cory's building.

Without really looking at her, he caught the sudden turning of her head. "You must have a good memory," she said, but he noticed that she made no immediate move to get out.

"Actually, I can't remember where I've left my checkbook half the time," he said. "But I still remember that you like to eat peanut butter and jelly sandwiches late at night."

"Good heavens!" Cory laughed, caught by surprise. "My guilty secret. And here I thought it was safe."

"I remember you had a dog named Tiger who bit you by mistake when you were nine," he went on. "I bet the scar is still there, isn't it?"

Slowly he reached out and took her left hand, pulling the glove off. He could feel her fingers trembling and wondered if it was just a result of leftover nerves from their slippery drive home, or if it was something more.

He'd had a more or less rational plan when he'd reached for her hand. If he could just remind her of how close the two of them had once been, maybe she'd give him the time he needed to find out what was wrong in her life now. But when he felt her slim fingers in his palm, and saw the sudden widening of those alluring blue-green eyes in the dimness of the car's interior, all his nice rational ideas deserted him. The only thing he could think of was holding Cory Vandergill in his arms again, and somehow convincing her that they could pick up the romance they'd abandoned ten years before.

His hands were shaky as he opened her palm and traced a faint line of the scar that was barely noticeable between her thumb and forefinger. "See?" he said huskily. "I thought so. I remember other things, too," he added, unable to stop himself. The rustle of his down jacket seemed loud as he leaned toward her.

"What things?" Cory's voice was soft, muted.

Buck lifted her hand to his lips and heard her whispered question end on a sudden intake of breath. "I remember how your skin felt," he said. The air was thick with desire; Buck could feel it invading his whole body. "Like cool satin. I've never forgotten it."

Cory couldn't suppress a low moan as he kissed her hand. His lips against the warm center of her palm made a direct connection to the center of her being. He drew her into his arms, slowly, persuasively, and Cory let herself go, closing her eyes.

"I remember looking at you at the taping of the show when we were fifteen," he went on. His deep voice was so close to her ear that she felt it as she would have felt a caress. "I'd been seeing you every year for five years, but all of a sudden it was like I'd never seen you before."

"I remember that moment," she murmured. "You'd been clowning around with Richard, and you just stopped for no reason and stood staring at me."

"You were wearing a navy blue plaid kilt," he said. "And a white blouse with a ruffle around the neck."

"Quite a memory you've got," she said. His mouth was so close to hers that they were barely whispering, their voices as light as the snow that was still feathering down outside. The windshield was half-buried again, hiding the two of them in a snowy cocoon.

"Want me to tell you what else I remember?" There was almost a roughness in his tone, but instead of going on, he lowered his lips to hers, and the flood of passion and memory that overwhelmed her was more eloquent than any words ever invented. He teased her lips open, waiting until she welcomed him further. And then, when his tongue met hers and their mouths melded warmly, hungrily together, she could feel a sudden urgency in his movements and a greater strength in the arms that pinned her to his broad chest. She was feeling the same explosion deep inside herself—a sudden admission of need and longing for each other.

His tongue embraced her, challenging her to answer him. And she did, in wordless sounds from deep in her throat. His hands on her hair, on her face, were intoxicating, fueling their mutual madness. It was as though they'd stolen a passionate moment from the past—the moment they'd first stepped into each other's arms and found heaven.

Cory raised her gloveless left hand and ran her fingers through Buck's thick brown hair. Touching him made her feel so warm and alive, she thought. Her fingertips brushed over the powerful muscles of his neck, and her heart seemed to surge inside her as she imagined exploring further, touching all of him, feeling him caressing the secret places of her body.

For an instant she let herself give in to the seductive picture his kisses were painting in her mind. The two of them had never pursued this powerful longing to its limits, although Cory had imagined making love with Buck a thousand times. She knew she should resist the crazy impulse that was carrying her, but for the moment, it was hard to remember why.

Then Buck lifted his head and spoke, and reality suddenly came back into focus again. "And to think," he muttered, "that I only came up here to talk to you about that damn show."

He obviously hadn't intended the words to break the spell, but for Cory that was exactly what they did. She forced in a deep breath and pulled herself away from his embrace. The mention of the television show brought back every misgiving she'd had about Buck's visit today, and then some.

"Buck, this is crazy," she said, wishing she could sound more in control of herself. "We can't let ourselves get carried away like a couple of teenagers here."

"I agree." He reluctantly loosened his hold on her. "Why don't we go inside and get carried away like adults, instead?"

The glint in his brown eyes were dangerously appealing. It was telling her all the things he really knew about her, and all the things he'd only imagined. But Cory made herself be firm.

"That wasn't what I meant," she said. "There's just no sense letting things flare up again like this. It was a dead end before, and it's even more of a dead end now."

Her words seem to surprise him. The seductive gleam in his eye faded, replaced by a harder look. "What makes you say that?" he demanded.

"Surely I don't have to spell it out for you. You want me to do this show so you can have another career success, and I don't know if I can do it." She pulled her glove back on, suddenly wanting to be anywhere but in this closed space with Buck.

He put a strong hand on her wrist as she reached for the door handle.

"It's not just the show, is it?" he asked in a low voice.

"Sure it is."

"I don't think so. If it was just a matter of business, you wouldn't be so upset now."

She knew there was no way to keep her emotions from surfacing. They were just too powerful. "It's not just business, and you know it," she said. "I just don't want to stir up memories of things that never should have happened in the first place."

"You mean us?"

She knew he was being intentionally blunt, and she decided to match him. "That's exactly what I mean," she said. "I don't choose to get my heart broken a second time, if that's all right with you."

"You weren't the only one who got hurt ten years ago."

"No, but I seem to be the only one who learned from the experience," she replied.

"Things are different now," he insisted, stubbornly refusing to loosen his grip on her wrist.

Cory gave a short, frustrated laugh. "Not different enough," she said. "Would you let go of me, please? Our business together is over."

His eyes narrowed, and he didn't let go. "I remember that, too," he said.

"What?"

"That grand-duchess air you used to use when you wanted to end a conversation."

"Grand-duchess! Look, Buck—"

"I'm sure it worked like a charm in your restaurant, Cory, but it isn't going to work on me. What are you doing for your birthday on Sunday?"

The sudden change of subject caught her completely off guard, and she blurted out the truth without thinking. "Ignoring it," she said. "Will you let me go now?"

Inexplicably, he did. With a long wordless look back at him, Cory got out of the car. She didn't say goodbye, partly because she had the unsettled feeling that the pushiest son of a gun in the National Hockey League had just started a whole new game.

Birthdays were definitely overrated occasions, Cory thought. In spite of the bottle of champagne she and Annie and another couple of friends had just shared, she still wasn't feeling in a celebratory mood. It had been nice of Annie to invite her over—even though she'd had to plead another appointment at three—but by the time she arrived home, Cory had already reverted to her earlier plan of ignoring her birthday altogether.

She knew much of her gloomy mood was because she'd spent the past two days—and nights—thinking about Buck. She hadn't seen him again, although she'd expected to. In fact, she didn't even know if he was still in Keene. But he was certainly making his presence felt in her thoughts.

The more she considered it, in her waking hours, the surer she was that she'd been right not to let things go too far. She reminded herself over and over again of how things had ended up the first time, and she knew there was a very good chance they'd turn out that way again.

The problem was that once she started calling up old memories, it was impossible to stop the tide, and she found herself reliving a part of her life she'd tried hard to forget. But *Five by Ten*, and all that went with it, was coming in loud and clear.

In the early years she'd felt like the odd one out on the show. The other four had such clear ideas of what they wanted to be, and her own idea of owning a restaurant some day had seemed pretty hazy to her at the time. She'd enjoyed the tapings and the mild celebrity status that came with being a part of a TV show, but it hadn't been a major part of her life.

Not until she was fifteen. That year something had started to happen between her and Buck. She hadn't understood it fully at the beginning, but over the next three or four years, *Five by Ten* had gradually come to be the highlight of her year, because it was a chance to see him. They'd always been friendly, but now there was a charged atmosphere whenever they were together, and she knew Buck felt it, too.

She could remember vividly the moment they'd first admitted their feelings for each other. They were nineteen years old, and just about to go their separate ways after the taping of the second-to-the last show. They'd never kissed, never had more physical contact than a casual brushing of hands when they happened to pass close by each other. Yet as they stood together in a quiet corner of the hotel lobby, waiting for the two cabs that would take Buck to the airport and Cory to the train station, she knew that the same thoughts of touching were filling both their minds.

"How soon do you know if you'll get a contract from a team?" she'd asked him, to fill the silence.

He'd seemed moody that day, but he answered her readily enough. "Should be in a couple of months," he said, shoving his hands deeper into his pockets.

"It must be pretty exciting for you."

He didn't seem nearly as enthusiastic as he'd been earlier, talking about his career prospects during the tapings. "Yeah, well, we'll see how things go. And what about you? Are you ready for your first year of cooking school?"

"Absolutely. Getting accepted was incredible enough but the full scholarship was icing on the cake."

She'd smiled at her own joke, but the look on his face was serious. "Cory, I just wanted to ask—" he began, then seemed to change his mind.

"Ask what?" she'd prompted gently.

He tried to summon his boyish grin, but it wouldn't appear. "Just whether you remember calling me a dumb jock about eight years ago."

"I remember. You'd just thrown Arlene into a swimming pool, as I recall."

"Well, I guess that *was* pretty dumb." He'd been struggling for nonchalance, but Cory could see the hunger in his eyes. "What I really wanted to ask is, do you still think I'm nothing but a jock? Dumb or otherwise, I mean?"

Cory's heart had started to beat faster, and she could see in his face what his words couldn't quite convey. "I'm not sure what to think of you as," she'd said honestly enough. "Maybe you should try to tell me more."

She already knew he was more comfortable with actions than with words. Without speaking, he'd reached for her, and she'd melted like a brook in springtime, only too glad to follow the feelings that had been building up inside her for so long. His kisses and the youthful strength of his athlete's body had been a dizzying confirmation of all the half-admitted dreams she'd kept hidden until now.

The year that followed had been one of the busiest, and certainly the happiest, that Cory had known. She became the acknowledged star of her class at culinary school, and Hector James, basking in her accomplishments, was eager to set her up in a restaurant in Keene. Her professional future seemed rosy, and as the year went on, she grew more and more involved with Buck. Not that they saw each other more than three or four times—his busy schedule wouldn't allow that—but they did manage to spend a couple of weekends together. And meanwhile Buck ran up prodigious long-distance bills and Cory wrote to him frequently. They hadn't done anything as concrete as make plans yet, but they both knew it was only a matter of time.

It was the memory of that final encounter, just before the last *Five by Ten* taping, that was keeping Cory awake nights ten years later. "That man never did know how to deal with reality," she muttered to herself as she stamped her feet in the vestibule to get the snow off her boots. She refused to let herself dwell on their traumatic breakup, having replayed it in her mind over and over in the past two days. At least it had reinforced her certainty that she'd been right not to let Buck too far into her life again.

That made it even more of a shock when she opened her apartment door and saw him reclining on her sofa as if he owned the place.

Cory blinked. After a moment's startled silence, she noticed that there were also balloons floating in the air. Dozens of them—green and yellow ones. She blinked again. The balloons were still there.

So was an enormous bouquet of daffodils and tulips on her dining room table. There was a cake in the center of the table. There was a present next to the cake. There were streamers everywhere.

And there was Buck with a wide smile on his face, getting to his feet and moving toward her.

"What on earth—" was as far as she got, before he put an arm around her shoulders and kissed her gently.

"Happy birthday, Cory," he said. His arms felt as strong as ever. He smelled clean and enticingly masculine. She'd never figured out whether that scent was something that came out of a bottle, or whether it was just pure Buck.

"How did you get in here?" she demanded, pulling back from his embrace.

"A little collusion with your landlady and your lawyer. Seems I'm not the only one who thought you shouldn't be allowed to ignore your birthday."

"So that's why Annie kicked me out at a quarter to three," she said, light dawning.

"Come on," he said. "You have to blow out the candles." He sounded quite at home playing host to her in her own apartment, and the way he was holding her so close to him was doing crazy things to her pulse. Feeling almost light-headed, Cory let herself be steered over to the dining room table, where thirty candles were burning brightly...on a cake shaped like a horn of plenty.

Cory took a deep breath, but not for the purpose of blowing out the candles. She looked up at Buck, but there was no change in his smiling, handsome face. Why was he doing this to her?

"Who told you about Horn of Plenty?" she demanded, pulling away from his embrace.

"What do you mean?"

"My restaurant. Someone told you the story, didn't they?"

"No one told me anything. And what does that have to do with—"

She gestured angrily at the decorated cake, with its brightly colored vegetables spilling out of the horn's open mouth. "Looks to me like you've been doing a little research, Buck," she said. "That might be a copy of the restaurant's logo."

He had his hands on his hips. "I don't know what you're talking about," he said.

"I'll just bet you don't. I suppose it's just a coincidence that you ordered a cake in this shape, huh?"

"I ordered it because of your connection with gardening, presumably for the same reason you called your restaurant Horn of Plenty. I had a hard time convincing the lady at the bakery that I really did want a Thanksgiving design."

Cory shook her head. "I don't know what you're trying to do, but whether it has to do with me or with *Five by Ten*, I can tell you it's not going to work."

"Cory, listen to me."

Cory could feel herself losing control of her temper, pushed to her limits by conflicting feelings for this man.

Remember the lesson you've already learned, her common sense told her. Don't let Buck take over your heart again.

She looked down at the cake and felt the sting from the association of the cornucopia and the scandal that had forced her to close her restaurant. Then she looked back at Buck, meeting his dark eyes defiantly. "You listen to me, Buck Daly," she said forcefully. "We have nothing more to discuss. I want you out of this apartment, and out of my life, in the next two minutes. Is that understood?"

Now he looked angry, too. "You're acting irrational," he told her.

"I'm sorry you think so." She shot him her best crushing glare. It didn't seem to make an impression. "And I'm sorry you went to all this trouble for nothing. But my mind is made up. I'm not having anything to do with you personally."

He was watching her through narrowed eyes. "Who said anything about having to do with me personally?" he asked.

"Nobody...yet. But you've sure been giving the impression that that's what's on your mind."

"If I have, I'm not the only one. The way you kissed me back the other night—"

This was getting far too dangerous for Cory's liking. She had to cut things off now, before they got into a wrangle that would cause them both more pain.

"That's enough," she said sharply. "If I gave you the wrong impression, I'm sorry. Maybe I got a little carried away."

"But—"

"Let's not argue about it, Buck." She was steering him to the door now. "Believe me, it's better just to stop things now, before we *both* get carried away again." She handed him his coat, and when he still refused to take the hint, she opened the apartment door and started down the stairs.

Throwing out a prizewinning pushy son of a gun was turning out to be harder than she'd anticipated. She got all the way to the bottom of the staircase before she realized that he wasn't following her. "Are you coming?" she demanded. "Or do I have to haul you down here by force?"

He was grinning now. "I'd like to see you try it," he replied.

"All right, so it was just a figure of speech," she grumbled. She refused to let her anger be weakened because of his charm. "But I'm serious, Buck. I want you out of my apartment."

"On one condition."

"What's that?"

"That you tell me why the idea of us getting back together makes you so nervous."

"Who said I'm nervous?"

"If you're not, then why are you trying to throttle the banister like that?"

"I'm angry, not nervous. And since you asked—" She tried to come up with a way to make her doubts clear to him, without giving away the emotions he'd stirred up in her. "I fell for you once in a big way, Buck. It would be very easy for me to do it again, if I let myself. But I just can't see that it would work, that's all."

At least he was starting down the stairs now, keeping his end of the bargain. Somehow, though, his approach wasn't calming her down any.

"Care to explain why?" he asked, almost casually.

"For the very same reasons it didn't work the first time," she said. She clung to the remnants of her anger, as if only that could protect her from the almost predatory look in his eyes. He was almost to the bottom of the staircase now, and

Cory found herself torn between the urge to back away from his muscular presence and the even stronger urge to move toward him. Standing her ground was one of the most difficult things she'd done in recent memory.

"Remind me of what those reasons were," he said. His voice was smooth now.

"Oh, come on, Buck. I'm sure you haven't forgotten."

"As I remember it, I proposed to you and you turned me down because you decided you'd rather come up here and run a restaurant."

Cory let out a frustrated breath. "That's only half of it, and you know it. What about you and that big-time career of yours?"

"Cory, I'd been offered a contract with an NHL team. Was I supposed to throw that away to come and live in a small town in New Hampshire?"

She could feel the old familiar tug-of-war starting in her stomach again. "Of course not," she said. "But I wasn't wild about the idea of seeing you once every three weeks, either. And it still doesn't appeal to me."

She saw him start to argue, but then, miraculously, he seemed to see the truth in her statement. He'd already admitted, after all, that his new venture was going to eat up a lot of his time and involve a lot of traveling. Cory took advantage of his momentary silence to open the door, letting in a blast of winter air.

With an effort she managed to conjure up the steely eyed look that had been so useful in getting rid of customers who'd had too much to drink. "I'll see you to your car."

She'd taken hold of his hand and was preceding him down the stairs before she realized she wasn't sure where his car was. He must have parked it out of sight as part of his surprise. Well, no matter. Seeing him to the door would just have to do.

She could tell he was resisting leaving. Holding on to his hand was like tugging the rains of a willful horse. But she got all the way down the front steps, feeling glad she was still wearing her coat and boots, when she realized that somehow, in spite of all her good intentions, the sensation of holding his hand had become pleasant instead of contentious. Very pleasant, in fact.

One look at his face told her he hadn't been going along with her plan to get him to leave. He'd just been thinking up his next move, and she had a feeling what it might be.

Thursday night's snow hadn't started to melt yet, and the gray late afternoon light was brightened by the snow on the lawns. Buck's face looked sharply etched. "What would you do if I just decided to stay around in Keene until you calmed down?" he asked her.

"I'd say that's your prerogative," she replied, "but you'd be wasting your time." She wished she had the strength of will to let go of his hand.

"And what would you say if I told you that I wouldn't consider it a waste of time? That even when you're angry with me, I'd rather be around you than anywhere else?"

Cory felt something in her throat constrict at his words, and she was shaking just the way she had as a shy nineteen-year-old. She forced herself to remember the way Buck was plunging himself into a new and all-absorbing career, and the way he wanted to use her and *Five by Ten* as a way to further that career.

"I just can't see this leading anywhere, Buck," she said unhappily. Finally she managed to pull her hand free. When she looked down at her fingers, they were trembling.

"Maybe you're looking too far ahead. What if you just look at the immediate future? Is there anything for us there?"

She knew he was using all the persuasive charm he possessed, and she made herself fight it. Buck had rampaged back into her life at a very vulnerable time: she was lonely and without the job she'd loved so much. And with his full-steam-ahead philosophy of life, he could very easily take over.

She knew that wasn't the way it should be. She reminded herself of Heck James and the way he'd let her down when the going got tough. The whole poisoning incident had left her feeling bruised and leery of trusting anyone—especially handsome hockey players who'd already broken her heart once.

Slowly, she shook her head. "Sorry," she whispered. "I don't think so."

All sorts of emotions were crowding in on her now. She felt the pain of her old parting with Buck, and the shock of seeing him again. Her anger and frustration at the way her career had ended mixed with the desire that wouldn't quite go away whenever Buck was near her. It was a confusing jumble of thoughts and feelings, and it added up to a powerful urge to get away from Buck's insistent probing, to somewhere quiet where she could think this through.

He was moving closer now, and she felt her pulse quickening with that instinctive attraction that both plagued and delighted her. She knew she couldn't get caught up in another embrace now, and she took a quick step backward, for safety.

Buck never stopped. "Cory, wait," he began, reaching for her.

Something in Cory gave way. "Leave me alone," she told him. Then, not stopping to consider that he was the one who was supposed to be leaving, not her, she turned around and started to run.

Four

———

She got a head start, and then she heard his boot heels on the pavement as he started after her. She picked up her pace, realizing how crazy it was to get into a foot race with a man who'd spent most of his life as a professional athlete. But it would be even more foolish to stop now, so she pushed herself to go a little faster.

At first she had no real destination in mind. All she wanted to do was outdistance those ringing footsteps behind her. He'd pushed her too hard, stirred up too many unsettling things. And he'd refused to take her obvious hints that she didn't want him to keep at it. Maybe it was ridiculous to be running like this, but at the moment Cory couldn't think of what else to do.

After a few blocks, Cory knew she was heading instinctively for the place she always went to when she wanted a long walk—a big, wooded park that was part of the Keene State College campus.

"Cory, wait!"

She heard Buck and slowed long enough to glance over her shoulder. She actually seemed to be keeping ahead of him.

"Forget it, Buck," she called back.

She couldn't hear if he answered; she was already running faster again. The sanctuary of the big park was just ahead, and she turned in its direction. Once she reached the jogging path, she took a quick breather and turned back to look at Buck. She'd definitely outdistanced him, she noted with surprise. And then she realized why.

He was limping badly, and even this far away, she could discern the pain in his face. He was hardly putting any weight on his right ankle, and the contrast between his gait and the athletic strength of the rest of his body brought her up short. She stepped back into view, and waited for him.

"I'm sorry, Buck," she said, as soon as he was within speaking range. "I forgot about your ankle."

He didn't say anything as he hobbled painfully toward her. She thought he must be furiously angry, but then she realized he was just out of breath from the effort of following her. She caught a flash of his boyish grin as he spoke.

"I forget about it myself, most of the time," he said. "But then, most of the time I'm not called on to run a four-minute mile."

"I wasn't that fast," she replied, and couldn't help answering his smile with one of her own. "Are you all right?"

"I will be after I've taken some weight off this ankle." He was standing close to her now, and unself-consciously she put an arm around his waist to help him. He was breathing deeply, and she could feel his strong, resilient muscles expanding and contracting under her hand.

"There are benches all along the path," she said. "Come on. It's just through the trees."

She felt as if everything had been turned upside down in the two minutes it took to reach the nearest bench. Until now, Buck had been the overbearing one, bullying and cajoling to get what he wanted. All of a sudden, he was surprisingly meek about leaning on her as they walked. She slid her arm a little more closely around him, not because he needed the extra support but because he was infinitely more attractive now that he'd stopped playing the heavy.

She stayed right next to him as he collapsed gratefully on the wooden bench. He kept his arm around her shoulders. "Feeling cold?" he asked.

She shook her head. "Are you kidding? That's more exercise than I usually get in a week. My blood's all warmed up."

So's mine, Buck almost added, but it has nothing to do with exercise. Just looking at Cory did that to him. The way her satiny dark blond hair—loose today, as it had been on Thursday—framed her face... In spite of the pain in his ankle, all Buck could think about was kissing her.

He managed to restrain himself, aware that the restraint was purely temporary. "Well, you run pretty fast for someone who doesn't exercise," he commented. "Or am I such an ogre that you couldn't wait to get away from me?"

"I don't think you're an ogre. And I wouldn't have run at all, if I'd remembered about your ankle," she said ruefully, looking down at it. "Does it still hurt very much?"

"It'll stop before long," he said, not wanting to let her know that it hurt like hell. "It's funny," he added, pulling her a little closer to his side. "I used to look at this ankle and think that two shattered bones had ended my whole life. And now it's not much more than a minor nuisance."

Holding her like this was the best way in the world to forget the pain, he decided. She felt so good nestled in the crook of his arm. Desire was crowding out everything else he should be concentrating on. He could almost taste the warm caress of her kiss, and feel her mouth opening to him. He was aware of both their hearts pounding in the sudden quiet of the woods, and he wondered if she was feeling the same excitement. Holding himself still with an effort, he let the silence go on uninterrupted until Cory finally spoke.

"I guess I owe you more explanation than I've been giving you," she said.

"Well, I think things might be clearer between us if you explained a little more," he said.

God, he loved that slight upward tilt of her eyes—it had always made her so mysterious, alluring. How could he sit and converse politely when she affected him this way? But he made himself do it. They definitely had things to sort out before he could let himself give in to the impulses that filled him whenever he was with her.

"All right," she said. "I'll tell you about it." She took a deep breath and looked away from him, at the low evergreens that were still mantled in snow. In the distance Buck could hear kids playing, but the path was deserted.

"If you've read about my career and my restaurant, then you know I'd made sort of a trademark out of using the best fresh produce, even in New England in the winter," she said. "It was one of the things that got me noticed. I had a great big garden behind the restaurant, and a greenhouse for the colder months. And I'd invented a lot of recipes that featured the things I grew. That's what I won the Innovative Young Chef award for."

Her eyes became pensive, and Buck suspected that reliving these memories was something she didn't allow herself to do too often. "And what went wrong?" he asked gently.

Another deep, reluctant breath. "It happened two and a half years ago," she said. "In the space of a week, eight people were hospitalized after they'd eaten at Horn of Plenty. They all had arsenic poisoning."

"My God."

Cory went on grimly. "The police and health inspectors traced the poison to vegetable dishes that they'd all ordered. Vegetables I'd grown myself in the restaurant garden."

"Did anyone . . . die?"

"No, thank goodness. But they were pretty sick for a long while. It was a bad time." Understatement of the year, Buck thought. It must have been slow torture, waiting to see if the poisoning victims were going to be all right.

She was looking curiously at him now. "I have to admit, I'm a little surprised you didn't hear about this," she said. "There was a lot of publicity when it happened."

"Two and a half years ago I was watching my career going down the drain," he said tersely. "I wasn't paying much attention to the news or anything else." He glossed over the thought of his own unhappy memories and turned back to Cory's tale. "Surely the police didn't think you were responsible for the poison," he said.

"You bet they did. At least, that's what they seemed to be trying to prove."

"Were you the only one who worked in the garden?"

"No. A couple of the other staff members used to help me with it. But suspecting them was as bad as suspecting me. They were all trusted friends."

"Then who would have done it?"

She turned anguished eyes to him. "Do you think I'd keep it a secret if I knew?" she replied. "I've been trying to figure it out for two and a half years, and I'm not any closer to finding out what really happened. All I know is that one week I had a phenomenally successful little restaurant, and the next month nobody would come near my cooking to save themselves. Not that I can blame them.'' Her voice was bitter, and so was the smile she tried to come up with. ''Maybe I could have built up the business again, but to be honest, I didn't have the heart to try. Or the money.''

''And that's why you don't want to get a job in another restaurant,'' he speculated.

''Right—assuming anyone would want to hire me. I just scrapped the whole thing and decided being a secretary would be a lot less painful.''

''It must have been hard as hell to give it up.''

''It was. I had a cookbook of my Horn of Plenty recipes half written, and I know it would have sold like the proverbial hotcakes. But selling a cookbook of vegetable recipes when your vegetables have just poisoned eight people—'' She stopped and looked away quickly.

Buck's mind was working busily, now that he'd bounced back from the initial shock of Cory's story. ''What about the other people on your staff?'' he asked. ''Was there anyone disgruntled, or—''

She held up a warning hand. ''Buck Daly, you sound like a paraphrase of the police investigation. Except that went on for months, and I heard every question you could possibly come up with, a hundred times.''

Buck instantly scrapped all the questions he'd been going to ask. ''I can imagine,'' he said. ''Just let me ask one more thing. The lawsuit you're in the middle of—that's because of the poisonings?''

''Yes. Six of the victims are suing me because they were sick for so long and because of loss of income and mental anguish and so on.'' She leaned forward, turning her face slightly away from him. ''Mental anguish! I could tell them a thing or two about that, not to mention loss of income.''

"If anyone's a victim in this thing, you are," Buck pointed out.

"I agree. And I hope the Supreme Court will see it that way, too. But Annie says my being a victim, too, is no guarantee that things will go the way I want them to."

Her eyes narrowed, a gesture that had always given her the elegance and mystery of a purebred cat. Buck knew she only looked like that when she wanted to keep her distance from someone or something. But on him, it had the perverse effect of making him want to hold her and kiss her until those impossibly aqua eyes softened again and looked back at him with the passion he knew she could feel.

"If you win the lawsuit, are you planning to open another restaurant?" he asked abruptly.

She turned her hands palms up. "I'd like to," she admitted. "But it's a question of finding financial backing."

"What about Heck James?" he asked. "Maybe he'd fund you again."

"It'll be a frosty day in Tahiti when *that* happens," she said. "I guess I might as well tell you the whole story, since I've started. I told you I'd gradually bought out Heck's share in the restaurant over the years. By the time of the poisonings, I was sole owner." She sighed. "I had to close Horn of Plenty temporarily after those people got sick. Once I reopened, business was so slow that I went through my reserves in no time, and I could see I wasn't going to have enough money to keep going if the slack period lasted more than a few months. Most restaurateurs aren't able to save much."

"You should have applied for a bank loan," Buck suggested.

"I did, but with the threat of a lawsuit hanging over me, I wasn't exactly a good credit risk," she said. "I hoped that

Heck might take a chance on me again, so I went to him and asked him for help."

"And let me guess—he turned you down." Buck's voice was gentle.

"Yes. Oh, he did it very nicely. He said his assets were tied up at the moment, and he just couldn't see his way clear to help me out. But the truth is, Heck only chooses to fund things that look good, and Horn of Plenty looked pretty bad at the time. It taught me a lesson," she added. "It made me very suspicious of people who want to borrow my name, or my expertise, when there's something in it for them."

Buck had a feeling those words were aimed directly at him. "What do you mean?" he asked sharply.

"I mean that Heck got a lot of free advertising out of financing Horn of Plenty in the first place. But when it was strictly a question of helping me through a bad time, I sure couldn't count on him."

The words "free advertising" struck a chord in Buck's mind. "Do you think I'm just another Heck James?" he demanded.

She studied him silently, then shook her head. Her hair swayed like a curtain. "No, of course not," she said.

Buck clenched his teeth. "If I were in your position and I wanted to open another restaurant, I'd do it no matter what people thought."

"It's not as simple as that, Buck."

"Why not? You're a great chef, and the poisonings weren't your fault. Sooner or later, people will realize those two facts, and you'll be back in business."

"That's crazy. If I did that, it would be like, well, like you breaking your ankle and then insisting you were going to keep playing hockey anyway."

She had pulled away from him and was standing up now, looking at him with eyes like an angry sea. Buck crossed his arms over his chest. He remembered this feeling so well. Why couldn't Cory take a long view once in a while, instead of letting herself get meshed in "what ifs?" like this?

"What I'm doing now is the next best thing to playing hockey," he told her. "And it's a whole lot better than giving up and getting a boring job somewhere."

"That's easy for you to say. You have enough money that you don't have to worry about paying the rent."

"Don't count on it."

"But you got paid a million dollars a year to play hockey," she pointed out.

"I also got saddled with alimony," he replied. "And in the early part of my career I had an agent who didn't choose the best investments for me. I'm not as rich as you seem to think I am."

The gloves were off now, Cory thought unhappily. The way they were glaring at each other reminded her painfully of the day they'd split up ten years ago. The same arguments were starting to resurface, and she was pretty sure they would lead to the same conclusion.

"Well, you've already admitted you got married in a hurry, to the wrong person," she said. She hoped her words would hit home, but it was still hard to watch the sting in his expression. "And your agent is another good example."

"A good example of what?" His voice was flinty.

"Of the way you get yourself into trouble by going at things too fast. And what about Sportsfix? Maybe it's not such a good idea to have staked your whole future on one project like that. What if it doesn't go as well as you hope it will? Surely your past experiences should have taught you that sometimes it's better *not* to go rushing headlong into things.''

"Actually, what it taught me is that I should trust my own judgment and not other people's,'' he retorted.

"Well, your judgment about my situation is away off the mark,'' she said. "You don't know the first thing about running a restaurant, or you wouldn't be making all these pronouncements.''

"I *do* know about making things work,'' he said hotly.

"Oh?'' She made herself stay deliberately cool, raising one eyebrow at him. "Is that why your marriage lasted only a year and a half? Or why you and I couldn't seem to come to an agreement ten years ago? Or—'' There was a stubborn obstacle in her throat, and she swallowed resolutely to get past it. "Or why we're fighting like this now? I'd say you know how to get your own way, Buck, but that's not the same as making things work.''

"You're confusing personal and professional tactics,'' he told her shortly.

"I don't think so. I'm just telling you I don't agree with the way you operate. You bulldoze your way past problems and tell yourself you've solved them. But in fact, you've just outmuscled them.''

Buck stood, ignoring the pain that still throbbed in his ankle. He'd started into this conversation so sure of himself, and somehow she'd managed to turn everything on its head.

"You know, this conversation is starting to have sort of a familiar ring to it,'' he said ominously.

Cory had been wondering when he would notice that fact. "I know,'' she said. "It may have been ten years, Buck, but this is what I meant when I said that if we got involved again, we'd run into exactly the same problems.''

She crossed her arms in an unconscious imitation of Buck's posture, and turned away from him. It was too difficult to keep watching his handsome face, and to feel the desire that welled up in her just from being close to him. Maybe if she concentrated on something else, she wouldn't feel so torn.

The trouble was, she couldn't escape the pictures rolling through her mind like old reruns. Her heart had thudded against her ribs in exactly this way ten years ago, when she'd had to face the possibility that she and Buck were going to have to go their separate ways. And now, although she seemed to be looking at the snow-covered trees in front of her, she was really seeing that hotel room in New York where they'd had their final confrontation.

It had been the morning before the last *Five by Ten* taping. They'd had a wonderful weekend, fired by their growing love for each other, and Cory had managed to quell all her misgivings when she'd tried, in her own mind, to figure out how their two lives were going to fit together. It wasn't until that last morning that she'd forced herself to bring up the awkward topic, and at first Buck had tried to gloss over it.

"We'll work it out," he'd said, buoyed up by his own enthusiasm. "We love each other—that's the main thing. The rest is just a matter of figuring out the details."

"But these are big details, Buck," Cory had insisted. "You're going to be based in Chicago. And my restaurant will be in Keene."

She still remembered the dismissive way he'd waved a strong arm in her direction. "I think you should set your sights higher than Keene," he'd said. "You're good at what you do, Cory. You should come to Chicago instead."

"I can't come to Chicago. My backer will only finance me if I set up shop in his hometown—*my* hometown."

"We'll find you another backer."

"It's not that simple. It's all very well for you to say I'm good at what I do, but the general public has no way of knowing that. This is a golden opportunity for me to prove myself, without going through years and years of working for other people first. It's just too good to turn down."

He'd made a short tour of the room, walking with that brisk impatience that characterized all his movements. "Well, then, I'll have to have a base in Chicago and one in Keene, I guess. I'm used to traveling. It shouldn't be a problem."

"Not unless you count seeing each other once very six weeks as a problem," she'd returned.

"You're being pretty negative, Cory."

"And you're not looking at the facts. You can't just shove past your problems like they were some big defenseman you want out of the way."

Oh, God, Cory thought, hugging her elbows a little tighter and forcing her gaze back to the present. Had things really not changed, at all?

She turned back to Buck, who'd put his hands into the pockets of his jeans. He, too, had been looking at the scenery, and she wondered whether that old scene had been replaying itself in his mind, as well.

"What are you thinking about?" she asked softly.

He seemed startled by the gentleness of her tone. He looked up, and she could see an unaccustomed vulnerability in his eyes.

"I was just wondering whether there could have been any way for us to work things out, ten years ago," he said. There was still a hint of anger in his voice. Whether it was directed at himself or her, Cory couldn't tell.

"I've wondered that, too."

"I couldn't do anything else."

"Neither could I." The frustration flared inside her again. Three meetings, and they'd already reached an absolute deadlock. "And we don't seem to be able to do anything else now," she added reluctantly. "So maybe now you'll see the sense in what I've been trying to tell you, Buck. It's not a good idea for you to stay around any longer, stirring up old memories that are better off forgotten."

She could see him fighting the idea, as he'd always fought the obstacles in his way. If she hadn't been struggling with her own emotions at the thought of having him walk out of her life again, she would have been interested to watch him grapple with the inevitable.

She might have known he wouldn't give up yet. He was silent for what seemed like a long time, and then he said unexpectedly, "What about *Five by Ten*?"

Cory shook her head slightly, startled by the change of subject. "What about it?" she asked.

"Are you going to do the show?"

"I told you. I'll think about it."

"Well, it's my job to see that you say yes."

"What do you mean, your job?" she stared more closely at him. He looked like someone who was plotting a strategy, and she had a feeling she was going to be on the receiving end of it.

"Well, not exactly a job, but something I've agreed to do."

"You mean you promised Theodore you'd get me to say yes."

"Right. And I don't like to back out of a promise."

"Does he know how I feel?"

"Yes. I called him after I saw you on Thursday night."

Reporting to headquarters, Cory thought. "And what did he say?" she couldn't help asking.

"He was surprised you were reluctant. He's laid a lot of the groundwork for doing a new show, and if he can't get all five of us to participate, he won't be able to go ahead. And he pointed out that the money you'll earn from *Five by Ten* could be very helpful in paying your legal costs."

"If I remember correctly, the stipend from the show is minimal."

"Well, here's another angle you may not have thought of. You've got a classic unsolved mystery here. Who put the arsenic in the vegetables? Crimes *do* get solved through nationwide publicity campaigns, Cory."

She considered the idea, then it occurred to her that he'd made this switch of subject just to throw her off the track. She'd raised a question he couldn't answer, and now he was putting her on the spot instead.

She looked into his eyes and said, "Seems to me we've gotten away from the main point here."

"Which point do you mean?"

"The fact that you and I are always at odds with each other. We always have been, and—" She couldn't say the words *we always will*, but surely Buck must know it by now. She felt as though a knife were twisting inside her, cutting through the happiness she'd once hoped for with Buck. It was as painful a sensation as it had ever been, and the sooner she got it over with, the better, she thought.

But Buck still had things up his sleeve. "You're right, it's a problem," he admitted. "But it's not the first problem."

"What are you talking about?" she felt her eyes narrow suspiciously.

"First of all, we've got to figure out what to do about *Five by Ten*."

"Why won't you just leave it at my saying I'll think about it?"

"Because I'm a pushy son of a gun." He grinned suddenly, catching her completely off guard. "Once we've worked that out to everyone's satisfaction, we can move on to other things."

Cory let her arms fall to her sides, completely out of patience with his bulldog way of doing things. "I don't know what to say to you," she told him. "You just can't see that we have one big problem, not a lot of little ones. And the problem is that your way of approaching life is just not something I can get along with."

She couldn't tell whether her words had actually made an impression. He was moving toward her now, an unpredictable smile on his face.

"And I know you have some difficulty with my way of doing things, too," she went on, less certainly. Why didn't he answer her? "So I just don't think—Buck, are you listening to me?"

In a split second he had closed the distance between them and pulled her into his arms. Immediately she was enveloped in his warm, masculine aura, and dangerously close to forgetting all the clearheaded arguments she'd just presented him with.

"I'm listening to the sound of your voice," he told her, his own voice rough against her ear. "And it's telling me some very different things from your words."

His lips traced the outline of her ear seductively, barely touching her skin, and Cory couldn't hold back a small cry in response. "You're saying some calm, sensible things," he went on huskily, and his breath in her ear seemed to seek out and caress unnamed places in her body. "But that voice of yours is telling me a very different story."

Her body felt so good held against his this way. She was helpless against the bond between them, she knew. "Buck, this isn't fair," she murmured. Her treacherous voice cracked a little, and suddenly she admitted to herself that he was right. What was the use of trying to send him away when she wanted him so fiercely?

"When you want something badly enough, you don't always fight fair." His words echoed her thoughts, and Cory gave up clinging to common sense, as if just for the moment they were on the same side in this.

Buck felt her change of mood, saw it in the way her eyes softened and heard it in the way she let out a slow, trembling breath as though she were letting go of something she'd clung to for a long time. He ran his fingers through her shiny hair, tilting her face up to his. He didn't care about subtlety or strategy anymore—and once his lips had tasted her sweetness, he knew he couldn't be subtle to save his soul. She tasted of a springtime that lasted forever—fresh, alive, and more than a little earthy beneath that elegant exterior.

He felt her mouth open against his, and he invaded it boldly with his tongue. He *knew* she wanted him, knew it by the way her tongue entwined with his, and the way her body fit against him as though she, too, were drowning in cascading images of the two of them together. He crushed her against his chest, feeling the tension in his muscles and thinking they might burst if he didn't find release in the unimaginable intimacy of making love with Cory.

He heard her moan, and detected the note of pleasure in the sound. The idea that she was as aroused as he was made his movements more urgent, and he slid his hands inside her unbuttoned down coat, outlining the inviting curves of her body through the cotton sweater she wore. He groaned as his fingers encountered the roundness of her breasts and the planes of her hips and thighs. Touching her like this brought even more potent images to his mind—images of exactly how their two bodies would fit together.

He heard voices in the distance and was vaguely aware that they were coming closer. "Skiers," Cory said, identifying the sound more quickly than he.

He lifted his head long enough to mutter something uncomplimentary about the skiers, and then claimed her lips again with a renewed intensity. He *had* to convince her to give them a second chance. The thought of walking away from Cory again caused him an almost physical pain, and he was vaguely aware that he'd wrapped his arms around her like iron bands, striving to hold her to him and overwhelm her by main force, if necessary.

Gradually though, he realized that now she was struggling against him and against her own response to his kisses. As the sounds of voices came closer, she put her hands up to his chest and pushed against him.

"Stop," she said. It was only a whisper of a sound, but he detected all her quiet stubborness in it. How could a woman be so strong and so yielding at the same time? Buck almost groaned as he lifted his head again.

That didn't mean he was ready to let her go. He stepped back a couple of feet, still holding her tight. "We'll just hide behind a tree," he said.

She frowned, pulling back from him as far as his powerful grip would allow, and decided she'd needed to get away from his damn-the-torpedoes philosophy *and* his bullying ways.

"Would you let go of me, please?"

She watched the inner struggle taking place in him, as he tried to decide whether to defy her or go along. Finally he released her, and Cory stepped back.

"Thank you," she said politely.

His grin wasn't quite as cocky as usual. "I hope I didn't crush you," he said. "Sometimes I don't know my own strength."

Cory regarded him levelly. "I'm not sure you know your own weaknesses, either," she said softly, almost to herself. But he caught the words, and his grin changed to a glower.

"What's that supposed to mean?"

Before she could reply, the family of cross-country skiers were upon them. "Hey, lady, do you know how to get to the arboretum?" one of the kids called to Cory. As she gave them directions, she stepped farther away from Buck, putting space between her body and his. If she could just keep her distance, she thought, she'd have a better chance of figuring this out.

When the skiers had glided off again, she looked up at Buck. She knew instinctively that his tactic was the exact opposite of hers: she wanted to stay away, while he was planning on getting closer, wearing her down by forcing her to admit the passion that was still so strong between them. That's an underhanded trick, Mr. Daly, she wanted to tell him, but instead she turned in the direction of her house and said, "I'm going home, where it's warm. Want some help getting to your car?"

Buck tried putting weight on his ankle, experimentally, and she could see him trying not to wince. "I think I'll sit a while," he said, taking a seat on the bench again.

"Is your ankle very bad?" She couldn't help feeling a little guilty about it.

"It'll be all right in a while. Anyway, I can use the time to think."

She didn't like the sound of that. "If you're making plans, they'd better be good," she warned him.

"Oh, they will be."

"Won't you be cold, sitting out here?"

"You seem pretty concerned about me all of a sudden."

"I just don't want to pick up my paper tomorrow and find the headline, Ex-NHL Star Found Frozen To Park Bench, that's all."

"Don't worry. Anybody who gets as far as being an NHL star has plenty of practice sitting on cold benches."

Still she hesitated, not sure why she hadn't obeyed her original instincts and gone. She'd been so angry with him this afternoon, and yet it was hard now to leave him behind. Then he looked up at her with that boyish grin, and she knew he'd been reading her mind, sensing the tug inside her that was keeping her standing on the snowy path.

His cocky smile was enough to do it. "Well, Buck," she said briskly, "it's certainly been a *different* sort of birthday party." And with that, she headed back across the white field, careful not to look back.

Five

———

Mondays and Tuesdays were always busy at the dentist's office, as if to make up for the slowness of Thursdays. The phone rang incessantly, and the waiting room was full. Usually Cory was happy to have lots to do, but this week the hustle and bustle was bothering her because she had some thinking to do.

Had she been right to walk out on Buck? That was the question that plagued her all the time she was setting up appointments and mollifying terrified five-year-olds with promises of balloons if they were brave in the dentist's chair.

She'd been sure of herself at the time, but now that she'd had some time to think it over, she wondered if she hadn't been too hard-line about the whole thing. She knew she had some good points, but so did Buck—particularly the point he'd proved so resoundingly with his kisses. Common sense was all very well, Cory decided at last, but you couldn't just ignore passion when it invaded your whole life this way.

There was no word from Buck on Monday or Tuesday, and Cory couldn't figure out what that meant. Maybe he'd gone back to New York, she speculated. He'd said he was right in the middle of trying to get his sports clinics launched.

If he was still around, why didn't he call? It wasn't like him. Cory considered the possibility that he was just giving her time to reflect, but that wasn't like him, either. By late Tuesday afternoon, partly because she couldn't stand the suspense and partly because she'd decided she owed Buck an apology for running out on him on Sunday afternoon, she made up her mind to call him.

She'd already reached for the phone during a brief lull in the afternoon's activities, when she realized she had a problem: Buck hadn't told her where he was staying. "Drat," she muttered, feeling her resolve beginning to crumble. Then she sat up straighter and told herself there was no reason why she couldn't be just as persistent as any hockey player ever born. Keene wasn't that big a place, and it was probable that Buck was staying at one of the hotels she'd recommended to him.

Three phone calls turned up three replies that no one named Buck Daly was registered there. Cory sighed. Now that she'd decided to call him, it was frustrating not to know where to find him. She put her finger on the phone's disconnect button, then lifted it again. She'd make one more quick call—to her lawyer.

Luckily Annie was in. "Sorry to bother you," Cory said. "I have a question for you, and I'd appreciate it if you would not, repeat, not, exhibit any curiosity about it."

"I'll do my best." Annie sounded as though she were smiling and, naturally enough, curious already.

"I gather you were talking to Buck Daly the other day," Cory said.

"About your birthday party? I sure was. That's one gorgeous man, Cory."

"Yes, well, he's also a missing person at the moment. He didn't happen to mention to you where he was staying, did he?"

"Sorry, he didn't. Oh, wait a minute. He did leave a phone number, because I wasn't in the first time he called. Let me see if my secretary still has it."

Luckily, Annie's secretary never threw anything away, and a couple of minutes later Cory was scribbling down Buck's hotel number on her desk blotter. Luckier still, Annie had to take another call immediately afterward, so Cory wasn't faced with any questions she wasn't sure she had answers to.

"But you owe me one," Annie warned her as they said goodbye. "No curiosity, indeed. I want to know what's going on, Cory."

You and me both, Cory thought, and glanced at her watch. It was almost five. She could make one more call on company time, she figured, and stay a few minutes late to make up for it. Mercifully, the crush in the office was thinning out by now.

Quickly, before she had time to talk herself out of it again, she dialed Buck's hotel and asked to be put through to his room. While she was waiting, trying to think of what to say to him, the office door opened and Buck himself walked in.

She was so surprised at first that she sat there looking from him to the telephone receiver, as though trying to figure out how she'd made him materialize simply by calling his number. Then she shook her head, laughing a little.

"You won't believe this," she said, "but I was just calling you."

He was wearing a bulky off-white sweater today, topped by a dark green down vest, and the contrast between the light-colored wool and his dark good looks made him more attractive than ever. His brown eyes were fastened on hers with that intensity that always made her heartbeat quicken. Cory wondered if he was unaware of the looks he was getting from the women sitting in the waiting room, as he threaded his way toward the reception counter. She was vaguely aware that another man, shorter and stockier than Buck, had entered behind him, but for the moment all her attention was riveted on Buck himself.

"I hope you weren't calling me with bad news," he said, leaning on the counter with that easy familiarity of his.

"No news at all, actually," she told him, lowering her voice so that the waiting patients wouldn't overhear them. "I just wanted to tell you I was sorry for walking out on you on Sunday. It wasn't the best way to deal with the situation, I guess."

He raised his eyebrows. "That counts as news, in my book," he told her. "And good news, at that."

"I wanted to thank you for the birthday present, too," she added. The present she'd found nestled next to the cornucopia-shaped birthday cake had been a silk scarf, painted in shades that might have been chosen with Cory's own coloring in mind—pale aqua and tan on an ivory background.

"Did you like it?"

"It's beautiful. I wasn't so sure about what you wrote on the card, though."

The card, nestled in with the scarf, had read, "To Cory— Happy Birthday. You can wear this when I take you out to the restaurant of your choice in New York during the tap-

ing of *Five by Ten*.'' The message had refueled Cory's anger on Sunday, and although she'd calmed down
considerably since then, she still wasn't about to let him get
away with pushing her this way, especially not when he was
grinning at her over the counter as though he was just
waiting to pull something new out of his bag of tricks.

His next words confirmed her suspicions. ''Well, at least
you liked the scarf,'' he said genially. ''And since you're
speaking to me again, maybe this is a good time to intro-
duce my friend here.''

He half turned, beckoning to the other man who'd come
in with him. The stranger stepped forward and held out a
hand to Cory. ''William de Vries,'' he said, with a friendly
smile. ''You can call me Bill.''

Cory shook his hand, wondering what on earth Buck was
up to now. ''And what can I do for you, Mr. de Vries?'' she
asked carefully.

''It's more a question of what Bill can do for you,'' Buck
amended. ''He runs a private detective agency over in
Manchester. He comes very highly recommended.''

''Buck, wait a minute—''

He cut her off with a wave of his hand. ''This is a great
idea, Cory. Just let me explain it to you.''

''If it has anything to do with Horn of Plenty—''

''Of course it does. Now, it's five o'clock. Why don't you
get your coat, and the three of us can go somewhere and
talk?''

She sighed again and spoke as quietly as she could. ''My
lawyer and I hired not one, not two, but *three* private investigators when the poisonings happened. I'll be happy to
show you their reports, if you like. They turned up a couple of leads, and the police followed up on them, but none
of it led anywhere. Believe me, there wasn't a stone left
unturned.''

Buck's eyes had turned stubborn. "Three investigators, huh?" he asked grudgingly.

"Count 'em, three."

She waited for him to draw his own conclusion, but he still hadn't replied by the time the evening receptionist arrived. While Cory explained a couple of messages and gathered her coat, boots and purse, she could see Buck deep in conference with his private eye.

She let them talk uninterrupted, guessing from the set of Buck's broad shoulders that he was reluctantly telling Bill de Vries his services wouldn't be needed. She caught his last words, though.

"I'll stay in touch," Buck said. "There may be something for you to do, after all."

The detective left with a sketchy wave in Cory's direction, and then Cory ushered Buck out into the hall, away from the stares of the patients for whom this little scene was a welcome diversion from thinking ahead to the dentist's chair.

"I'm grateful that you care about my situation," she said when they were finally alone. "But did it ever occur to you to call and let me know you were arranging that? Why do you keep charging around like a bull in a china shop?"

"Is that what I'm doing?" he said lightly, not seeming to take her seriously.

"You bet it is."

"You did point out that the poisoning scandal is what's keeping you from doing Theodore's show. I figured if I could help clear up the mystery..."

He spread his hands wide, smiling at her as if daring her to get mad at him.

"Let me get this straight. You're planning to find my poisoner and take away my objections about *Five by Ten*?"

"Right. And that's not all."

She almost didn't want to hear the rest, but she couldn't help asking, "And what else?"

"I'm planning to change your mind about me, too. About us, I should say."

He'd made no move to come closer to her or touch her in any way. Yet the thought of his kisses—and more—crowded instantly into Cory's mind.

She shook her head, forcing herself to concentrate on the real issues.

Hiring a private detective without consulting her was so typical of the brash way Buck did things. Surely he could see that, she thought.

Apparently he didn't. "I'd like to see those reports you mentioned," he said. "Do you have them at home?"

Cory hesitated. Inviting him to her apartment was too much like lighting the fuse on a time bomb. But maybe she didn't have to let him in—and surely the thick stack of reports she'd accumulated would absorb his attention so much that he wouldn't have time to deal with the more private matters between them.

"Yes," she said. "I'll be happy to lend them to you, if you promise to give them back."

"Scout's honor," he said, and held the front door open for her. The air outside was icy, with no January thaw in sight, but Cory had never minded the cold so much on clear nights like this, when the winter stars shone with a hard, brilliant light.

She could hear the packed snow crunching under Buck's tires as he drove her the few blocks she usually walked to and from work. They were silent as they drove, and when they reached Cory's building, she said quickly, "Wait here. I'll get the reports," before he could wangle an invitation to go inside.

She didn't wait to see how he took the obvious hint, and hurried up the stairs as though she didn't quite trust him to stay in the car. The reports were on the desk in her bedroom; she'd been studying them only last week, when Annie had called to discuss the pending court case. As always, the sight of the bulky pile of paper made her insides churn nervously with memories of the past scandal and trepidation about the lawsuit still to come. She shoved the reports into a large manila envelope and almost ran back down to the street.

Buck was still in the driver's seat, with the dark green car idling quietly. He seemed in no hurry about anything.

"There you go," she said. "And I hope you don't get insomnia from reading them."

He eyed the envelope. "More likely to *cure* insomnia," he speculated. "Why don't you give me a quick rundown of what they found out?"

Cory paused, then decided there couldn't be any harm in it. She slid back into the passenger seat.

"All three of them fastened on one person as a likely suspect," she explained. "I had hired a new waiter shortly before the poisonings, but he turned out to be such a dud that I had to fire him. I'd only taken him on in the first place because the business was booming and we were desperate for staff."

"So it might have been revenge for being fired?"

"Well, it was a possibility."

"Why didn't it pan out?"

She felt the old familiar frustration and helplessness starting inside her again. "They couldn't find the guy or any trace of him. He called himself Andy Vail, but that was probably an assumed name. Seems he was sort of a drifter."

"Did he come with references?"

"No, but he said he'd had experience, and he was very personable, at least at first. His story was that he was working his way across the country and wanted to stay in New England through the ski season. Lots of kids do things like that, so I decided I'd give him a chance."

The look on her face told Buck how bitterly she'd regretted that impulse. "How long before you fired him?" he asked.

"Ten days. Look, Buck, it's all in the report, and I really don't enjoy talking about it, all right?"

Now there was a definite edge to her voice, and Buck put the envelope into the back seat without pushing her further. The private investigator had only been one part of his new plan. For the other part . . .

"Let's go skating," he said, with no preamble, and was heartened to see her frown vanish, wiped clean by surprise.

"Skating! Where?"

"There must be lots of places around here."

"Rinks, you mean?"

"Actually, I was thinking of ponds and lakes."

"Well, there are a couple of good places. But I don't have skates. And my ankles are pretty wobbly."

"No problem." He reached into the back seat again and pulled out two pairs of ice skates. "Size seven and a half, right?"

"How on earth did you know that?"

"I have my methods. As for your ankles, you're welcome to lean on me."

"What about *your* ankle, Buck? It seemed so painful the other day—"

"It's fine if I warm it up properly. And if I don't try anything fancy, like running at top speed down an icy street."

"I really am sorry about that, you know."

"It's all right," he said lightly. "Tell you what. Instead of an apology, I'll accept a promise that you won't run away from me again, all right?"

She considered it silently and finally nodded. Her face was serious, elegant, her gaze level with his. He'd told himself that touching her only started off uncontrollable fireworks inside him, that it wasn't time for that yet, but he couldn't help leaning over and kissing her. Her lips, faintly glossy with a pale peach lipstick, seemed eager for his kiss, and that thought made his heart beat faster. Her subtle scent enveloped him, making him think of honey and violets at the same time.

He covered his feelings by buckling up the seat belt he'd undone and shifting the car into gear. "All right," he said. "You're the guide. Where's the best pond?"

"Down to the end of the street," she said without hesitation. "And then left. And Buck—"

He turned to look at her. There was a slight smile in her eyes.

"Promise me you won't laugh at my skating."

"If I dare to do such a thing, I promise I'll try to make a soufflé and let you laugh at me in return. Okay?"

"Okay." She was laughing already as he steered the car away from town.

The spot was secluded and very quiet. To reach the pond, they had to push through low-hanging boughs of balsam and birch trees. The result was worth it: the pond's surface, frozen hard and with just a skim of snow over the ice, was untouched and inviting. Cory and Buck wasted no time in lacing up their skates, leaving their boots behind on the shore.

"Make sure you warm up that ankle now," she said, as they glided hand in hand onto the ice.

"Yes, ma'am," he assured her. "Don't worry. I've been through enough physical therapy to know just how it goes."

They moved slowly across the pond, with the chilly early evening air biting their faces. Cory held tightly to Buck's hand, feeling his strength supporting her as her muscles slowly reminded themselves how skating worked.

She knew they had a lot of important things to discuss, but somehow she didn't want to bring up the subjects they'd fought about on Sunday. It was too pleasant just to glide alongside Buck, enjoying the silent evening and pretending there were no complications in their feelings for each other.

"Tell me about your accident," she said impulsively, as they rounded the pond for the second time. "How did it happen?"

He gave a quick shrug as though he didn't like to talk about it. "I'd busted this ankle when I was a kid," he said, "and it had always been my weak spot. One season I took a hard hit, and landed on it all wrong. That strained it, and it didn't recover completely in time for the next season. I played anyway, but it acted up pretty badly, and then one game against Toronto I slid into the boards and broke the thing into a million pieces." He grinned at his own exaggeration. "At least, that's what it felt like."

"I bet." Cory looked up at him. His thick dark brown hair was blown back from his forehead, and his heavy brows were drawn together. "So you had surgery to try to fix it?"

"Yeah. What a waste of time *that* was! I went through the whole gamut of doctors and therapists. Hell, it took me a year before I could even walk without a cane."

"You barely limp now," she commented.

"You're right—except when I have to chase someone." She saw the quick flash of his smile, and then his face became serious again. "The upshot of all of it is that I ended up with a lot of experience about sports injuries. It's a field that's advancing all the time, and there are lots of treatments now that are more effective than the ones I got. As I've said already, if I can franchise sports medicine clinics in lots of smaller cities and towns, it means lots of athletes will have a shot at treatment that could save their careers."

Cory was aware of the tension in her body, as she waited to see whether Buck was going to let his enthusiasm for his new project run wild again, intruding the real world into this private moment together. Just for the moment, she was perfectly content to let things ride, listening to the ringing of their blades against the ice and enjoying their closeness, and the unexpected thrill of being pulled along by his muscular strides.

Miraculously, Buck seemed to have come to the same conclusion. Instead of continuing his lecture about Sportsfix, he subsided into silence, and they made another full circuit of the pond before he spoke again.

"Do you have plans for dinner?" he asked casually.

"Not really."

"Want to have it with me?"

"Sure."

"There seem to be a lot of interesting little restaurants around here," he said. Now his casual air was a bit too obvious. She could see where he was heading, and she realized his silence had been just a ploy to give him time to think.

"Well, a college town is usually a pretty good place to eat," she said neutrally.

There was another pause, and then he said, "The New York restaurant scene really seems to be hopping these days."

"The New York restaurant scene is *always* hopping," she corrected him. "New York is food heaven, after all."

"Ever think of moving back there?"

"All the time." A stranger, overhearing them, might well have thought they were just chatting about nothing in particular, but Cory knew better.

"I meant, moving back and opening a restaurant."

She shook her head. "I'd love to," she said honestly. "But I can't even afford to reopen in Keene. New York is far beyond my budget now, and maybe forever."

"But you'd do it, if you could?"

It was a question she'd barely allowed herself to speculate on, but she was almost glad Buck had posed it for her. It forced her to look squarely at just what *was* in the future for her.

"With enough backing, yes, I would."

To her surprise, Buck made a frustrated motion with his free hand. "In other words, if there was no risk involved, you'd be happy to take the risk," he said. "You'll never make your dreams come true that way, Cory."

"Buck, running a restaurant is a very tricky financial proposition at the best of times. I'll spare you the figures on the percentage of new places that close after the first year, but believe me, they're not encouraging."

"How many of those are run by graduates of one of New York's best schools?" he demanded.

"Some. And I'm willing to bet that none of the ones that succeed are run by chefs suspected of being poisoners."

"What if you win the lawsuit? Then you won't be suspected any more."

"If I win the lawsuit, things might be different. But I'm not letting myself build up a lot of false hopes about it."

"Or a lot of real hopes, either, I'd say."

"You *have* said it, Buck. More than once."

He stopped suddenly, and she wobbled as she was cut off in midstride. She couldn't help careening into Buck's broad chest, and she knew he'd positioned himself so that she would do just that. She could feel the flicker of desire surfacing again, and suddenly their clasped hands meant much more than just a way to stay together while they skated. Cory could see the puff of Buck's breath when he spoke, and it reminded her of the way her skin had felt when he'd kissed her.

"Well, you're not done hearing it," he said, sounding almost threatening. "I'm not going to let you give up on your career, or on the idea of doing Theodore's show. Or on you and me, for that matter."

Frustration and desire were battling inside her now, in a familiar tug-of war. "Stop doing that!" she ordered him, pushing away from him with more agility than she'd thought she possessed. "Can't you see it's not going to work if you keep demanding things this way? Maybe we can work something out, Buck, but this isn't the right way to go about it."

She was a little less steady now, skating without Buck's supporting hand.

He followed her almost immediately, gliding beside her with easy strokes that made him look more athletic than ever. Maybe he was never going to score fifty goals a season again, she thought, but he would never lose that ease on the ice. His strong body moved like a finely tuned machine, and she couldn't stop herself from watching the way his strong thighs moved under his jeans. His upper body, strong and hard, barely moved as he skated.

"Did you mean that?" he asked suddenly, and once again she nearly lost her balance, caught off guard by his question and the quieter voice he used to ask it.

"I meant all of it," she said. "Which part weren't you sure about?"

"The part about there maybe being a way we can work things out."

Cory felt short of breath, and she tried to tell herself it was just because of the unaccustomed exercise. She knew, though, that her heart was pounding for more erotic reasons than mere aerobics.

"Yes, I meant it," she said, trying to sound crisp. Instead she sounded uncertain.

His skates made a harsh grinding sound as he spun into another sudden stop. This time, though, he didn't give her a chance to get away, and she felt herself being drawn into his arms, against that broad chest. Her heart was beating crazily by now. She leaned back in his arms, looking up into those penetrating brown eyes, and said, "I don't know why, but I really did mean it."

Her reply seemed to satisfy him. She saw his lips curve briefly into a smile, and he murmured, "I know why." Then he was pulling her even closer, close enough that she could feel his heart pounding. "This is why," he said, so softly that his words were no more substantial than the breath of air that accompanied them.

This time, Cory didn't even try to tell herself this was a mistake. What willpower she had was dazed to its limits by the things Buck Daly made her feel. Although she was still looking deep into his eyes, she was aware of everything around her—the surface of the pond like a snowy blanket, the brittle light of the stars, the motionless trees. The place had an enchanted atmosphere tonight, she thought. It was far removed from the rest of the world, and when Buck

kissed her, first very softly on her forehead and then on her
cheek, she felt like a very different woman from the one
who'd tried so hard to resist him.

He was kissing her other cheek now, warm and knowing, and then his lips found the base of her ear and nuz-
zled it seductively. Cory shivered inside her winter coat and
heard her own pleased gasp.

He seemed to have been waiting for that sound. She
heard him murmur in reply, like a big cat purring. She was
hungry for his kisses, anticipating the smoothness and intimacy of his tongue against hers.

But he kissed every part of her face and neck except her
mouth, and Cory had a confused feeling that he was toy-
ing with her, building up her own excitement to the point
where she'd have to admit the strength of what he stirred in
her.

He planted a trail of tiny kisses along the curve of her ear,
and the living, breathing nearness of him made her own
breath catch in her throat. He pulled off one of his gloves
impatiently and raised his hand to outline her face, his
gentle fingers feathering over her cheekbones and the eyelids she'd closed almost involuntarily. She was lost in a
warm, dark world of tiny sensations, each hooked to a part
of her that was throbbing now with unsatisfied desire. She
knew for a certainty just what his caresses were telling her:
he could touch every part of her like this and make her feel
things she'd never felt before. And she knew he was absolutely right.

"You're so beautiful, Cory," he was murmuring, exploring her high cheekbones and small chin with his fingertips. "Just like the fairy princess come to life."

So he'd had the same thoughts she had about the magic
in the air around them. She opened her eyes, smiling lan-

guidly at him. "Most fairy princesses don't have to work in dentists' offices," she said.

He smiled in return. "*All* fairy princesses have to do something unpleasant," he replied. "You know, scrubbing castle floors or something—not too different from typing ten words a minute for a living. Until they break the spell."

His brown eyes were dancing at her, and his white teeth showed in a smile. "I know a few spells of my own," he told her.

"I'll just bet you do." She raised her hands to his neck, wishing she wasn't wearing gloves. She wanted to feel the warmth of his skin and run her hands over his impressive body. She wanted to make him gasp with need, as he'd already done to her.

"These spells of mine don't work outdoors though," he was continuing, still smiling in that way that made him so irresistible. "You'll have to come back to my place with me, if we're going to try them."

"That sounds suspiciously like 'Come up and see my etchings,'" she teased him.

Something in her smile seemed to have told him how much ground he'd just gained, and he was smart enough not to waste any time pressing his advantage. He kissed her again with a maddening sureness that left no doubt how much he wanted her, then he said, "Come on. Let's go and get some dinner, and then we'll see if I can drum up some etchings to show you."

Six

They ate dinner at a small Mexican restaurant near the university. Even on a Tuesday night the place was busy, but Cory and Buck barely noticed the crowds of students around them. They ate with appetites sharpened by cold air and exercise, and found that for the moment, they'd managed to recapture some of the old camaraderie they'd shared before they'd complicated things by falling in love.

"I really didn't think one person could eat that many burritos," Cory said, looking in awe at his empty plate.

"I'm just a big, hungry boy," he told her, putting down his napkin. "You did pretty well yourself."

"So who's counting?" Cory smiled. "How do you eat so much and stay in shape?"

"You've got it backward. It's the staying in shape part that makes me so hungry."

After dinner they got back in Buck's car. Following their bantering over the meal, the drive was strangely silent. It was as if both of them had recognized that their relationship had moved forward in some indefinable way, and they were trying to adjust to the change.

If only to break the quiet, Cory asked, "So why did you pick the hotel where you're staying, instead of one of the places I'd recommended?"

"I wanted a little more privacy," he explained. "So I found a hotel that also rents out little ski cabins. I'm in one of those."

"Sounds pretty cozy," she commented. "What did you want all this privacy for?"

"Well, I have a lot of work to do on Sportsfix," he said seriously. "It's sort of a bad time for me to be away from New York, with the clinics just getting set up and all. So I have to be on the phone a lot, and I have a fair bit of paperwork to do. I just figured I'd work better in a quieter place."

"When are the clinics actually scheduled to open?" she asked.

"Well, we're aiming for fall. That way, if *Five by Ten* airs this spring the way Theodore's planning, we'll have some lead time on our major advertising thrust."

Cory found she was holding her breath, waiting to see whether he was going to let himself get caught up in the subject again. To her relief, he didn't, if only because they'd reached the turnoff for his hotel.

The cabin was as private as he'd described it, an open-plan building with one big room encompassing a king-size bed, small kitchen and a living room with a fireplace.

"Does the fireplace work?" she asked, as Buck closed the door behind them.

"It sure does. There's even a woodpile by the back door of the office. It's a little chilly in here, isn't it? I'll go and get some more fuel."

He was back in two minutes with his arms full of fire-wood, and soon had a fire going.

"Not bad," Cory said. "And here I always thought you were a city kid."

"I spent my summers at a hockey camp up in northern Michigan," he replied. "All us city kids got pretty good at lighting fires, mostly just to keep the bugs away." He stood and surveyed the big room. It was surprisingly homey, he'd found, with its color scheme of white and tan and the thick carpet that invited you to take your shoes off. He nodded toward the kitchen at the opposite end of the room.

"Don't ask me why I got a place with a kitchen," he said. "Even making instant coffee is a challenge for me."

Cory surveyed the kitchen utensils with a practised eye. "Making anything *but* instant coffee would be a challenge with tools like those," she said. "They never seem to sharpen the knives in places like this."

"Probably afraid you'll cut yourself and then sue them for all they're worth."

He'd meant the words as a joke, but the instant they were out of his mouth he realized how they must sound to Cory. Just as they'd finally managed to get off the subject of her lawsuit and ruined career, he thought, annoyed at his tacklessness.

"If you'll give me a minute to get my foot out of my mouth," he added hastily, "I'll retract that statement."

But the laughing sparkle in her eyes had died, and she looked serious again. Her face had regained that slightly regal expression that he'd always found so alluring, and he knew now that it attracted him because it always made him want to chase it away, to fight through Cory's practised elegance.

She'd brought the detectives' reports in with her, he noticed. She was holding the thick manila envelope in front of her now, like a shield. "Maybe we should get to work," she said briskly. "We were going to discuss these reports, after all."

So much for etchings, he thought regretfully. Well, he'd just have to work at recapturing that mood of magic they'd shared earlier this evening.

He sat down next to her on the sofa by the fireplace and watched her take the reports out of the envelope. "I guess we should begin at the beginning," she said. "This is what the first guy we hired turned in. Do you want to go through it yourself?"

"Why don't we flip through these together?" he said. "That way you can point out what's important and what's not. Otherwise we'll be here for days."

His dark eyes had a suspicious flicker in them, Cory noticed, and she had to wonder whether his suggestion was just a ploy for the two of them to end up sitting close together on the comfortable sofa. Now that she was actually alone with him in his cabin, she was strangely nervous, as though she'd taken a step she wasn't quite ready for.

She was constantly aware of Buck's nearness, especially when he bent his head to look closely at something, and his dark hair almost brushed her cheek. It was impossible to ignore the scent of him, that warm masculine smell she knew so well.

"So we've got a fairly detailed description of this Andy Vail," he was saying, and she had to make herself concentrate on his words.

"Yes. That composite drawing looks a lot like him. Unfortunately, it also looks a lot like a lot of other people."

"I can see that." He squinted at the drawing that the detective had patched together from the Horn of Plenty staff's descriptions. "How many states did they look for him in?"

"We could only afford an extensive search here in New England. There just wasn't the money to check records all over the country. The second detective tried some spot checks in a few major cities, but nothing turned up."

Instead of looking at the typed pages, her eyes strayed over and over again to the way his blue jeans were held taut over his powerful thigh muscles. His leg was touching hers on the sofa, not aggressively, but she was finding it disturbingly sensual all the same.

They spent an hour giving most of the material a cursory glance and then Buck put down the last report and leaned against the padded back of the sofa. "Well, I'd say your detectives did a good job with what they had," he said.

"They came highly recommended," she said. "But there just wasn't much in the way of clues. And I'm afraid the trail must be just about cold by now, so I can't see any earthly use in hiring yet another detective."

"Much as I hate to admit defeat, you may be right," he acknowledged.

"Well, run up the flag," she said, and he saw a hint of her earlier sparkle returning to her blue-green eyes. "Buck Daly has just conceded a point."

"I realize it doesn't happen often." He smiled back at her, and reached out a hand to brush her shoulder. "Just be warned that when it does, it usually means I expect to gain some ground somewhere else."

"At least you're honest about it." Cory couldn't help responding to the way his hand was massaging her shoulder. She knew it was only a prelude to more. "And what do you expect to gain this time?"

He shifted his weight, moving a little closer to her. "A reward for sitting this close to you for an hour without touching you," he murmured. His arm was around her now, and Cory felt herself drawn toward his strength even before he pulled her to him.

He'd taken off his sweater once the fire had warmed the room, and Cory could see the nearly black hairs at the open collar of his plaid shirt. She lifted her hand, running the fingertips over the base of his neck. It was like touching a low-voltage current; her fingers tingled at the sensation of those curling hairs on her skin, and the rest of her began to respond as well, when she saw his pulse beating in the little hollow of his collarbone.

He was pulling her into his arms now, kissing her. His mouth moved in slow circles against hers, telling her they had all the time in the world to enjoy each other. She parted her lips and their mouths merged hungrily.

She slid her fingers through his hair and down over the broad base of his neck again. His muscles felt hard and springy. "It's just as though we were never apart," she whispered, almost to herself. She remembered so vividly the delight of exploring Buck's athletic body with her hands.

"Maybe we should forget we ever *were* apart," he answered. Deftly he flicked open the top two buttons of her high-necked lavender blouse. She could feel the warm shadow of his breath surrounding her.

"We can't just forget about it, Buck."

"Sure we can. We can start over, from the beginning."

The beginning, for them, had been just like this, she remembered. This dazzling lightness, this brilliant flash of certainty that they were meant for each other. And this desire that made the blood race. Need was rapidly taking her over, body and soul.

She found herself wanting to undo the buttons on Buck's shirt, to see him without his clothes as she'd always fantasized. She stroked his shoulders and the hard planes of his chest, and pictured the powerful muscles she knew must be there.

Her caress had an explosive effect on him, as if nothing could excite him more than her desire for him. "Oh, God," he groaned. He pulled open his shirt himself and clasped her against him, letting his hands explore all her curves as he kissed her. Cory shifted in his grasp, moving mindlessly in response to the way he smoothed his hand over the line of her thigh and then moved upward to enclose the roundness of her breast. His thumb glanced over its hardened center, and the intimacy of the gesture shot her pulse rate off the top of the scale. Behind her closed eyelids she could see a shimmering light, and she could almost hear a ringing in her ears.

Almost, nothing. Cory opened her eyes suddenly, aware that there was a sound coming from somewhere in the room and that Buck was responding to it, too. He relaxed his grip slightly, and they both sat up.

"Damn," Buck said harshly, pushing himself to his feet and striding toward the bed. "I forgot I set this."

"This" was a small alarm clock by his bed. It was beeping insistently, not ringing, and when Buck slammed his hand down on top of it, the noise stopped.

The silence seemed very sudden. Cory had been swept up in a whole galaxy of inner sounds, all pulsing to the beat of her heart, and it was a shock now to hear nothing but the quiet crackling of the fire. She sat up a little straighter and watched Buck returning to the sofa. Before he could sit down again, she stood up and faced him.

"Do you always set your alarm for nine-thirty at night?" she asked casually.

"No. This is a special occasion." When she didn't answer, he went on rather reluctantly, "There's this doctor on the west coast I've been trying to hire for one of my

Sportsfix clinics. The guy would be a big draw, but the problem is he's so busy I can't ever get hold of him. He said tonight at nine-thirty our time would be a good bet to find him at home." He shrugged, looking apologetic.

Cory looked at the bedside phone. "Are you going to call him?" she asked.

"Hell, no. I've got too many other things on my mind besides Sportsfix right now." He reached out for her again, but Cory sidestepped him deftly. Now that her brain was clearing a little, she wondered if it was such a good idea after all to let things move this fast with Buck.

"Maybe just at the moment," she said cautiously. "But in general, you're pretty involved with it, aren't you?"

Reluctantly, he nodded. "Sure I am," he said. "It's a big part of my life. But so are you, Cory. I don't see that the two things have to be mutually exclusive."

Cory shook her head. "That's not the problem," she said. "It's more than that. It's—it has to do with what you said a little earlier, about us starting again at the beginning. We can't do that, Buck. We still have things to resolve. And that's why Sportsfix worries me. It looks to me as though you're throwing your whole self into another brand-new career, and I'm just not sure there can be room for me in your life, as well."

"Does that mean you *want* to be a part of my life?" She saw the hope flash in his dark brown eyes, and felt that little jolt of attraction between them. They'd been so closely connected, for so long.

Still, she hesitated before answering. "I want us to be a part of each other's lives," she said at last. "And I just don't see that happening yet."

"It can happen," he assured her. "Once this big opening push at the clinics is over with—"

She held up a hand to stop him. "Then there'll be something else," she said. "I know you, Buck. You create a whirlwind no matter what you're doing. We have to figure out how to deal with this situation, right now, before we look any farther ahead."

He took a turn around the room, as though anything was easier than standing close to her without touching her. In front of the fireplace, he paused.

"You're saying you want me to fit into your life as well as fitting yourself into mine, is that it?" he asked.

"That's exactly it."

"That's sort of a problem."

She knew exactly what he meant. "Right again," she said. "My life is very up in the air at the moment. I can't make predictions about what I may be doing even six months from now."

"You're telling me we have to deal with the situation we find ourselves in right now, but at the same time you're putting me on 'hold' while your lawsuit straightens itself out."

"That's not my fault, Buck. Blame the court schedule, not me."

"I'm not blaming anyone. I'm just saying it's a difficult situation, that's all."

"Amen to that." She sat down again and sighed. "I feel as though we're stuck in a time warp, Buck. It's just the way it was before. We're involved with each other, but somehow we can't seem to take it any further than that."

The glint in his eyes now was almost dangerous, as though he'd taken her words as a challenge. "There's one major difference between this time and last," he corrected her.

She expected him to point out that this time, she had no career of her own to stand between them. She was prepared to argue, but his next words surprised her.

"The difference is that last time, I didn't know what it was like to live without you," he almost growled. "And now I do. And it's not something I intend to do any more of, if I can help it."

Their eyes had locked, and Cory could feel that pervasive hunger growing deep inside her again. With each new admission of how he felt about her, Buck was breaking down the things her common sense had told her were true.

She was still mulling over his last statement when the phone rang. Buck moved as though a spring had uncoiled inside him, and picked up the phone beside the bed.

"Hello?" he barked.

She couldn't tell from his tone whether he was angry or glad at the interruption. But after a moment, his voice became friendlier. "Oh, hi, Elaine. I forgot you were going to call." There was a brief pause, and then he said, "No, I haven't gotten hold of him yet. I haven't had a chance." A longer pause. "No, I realize that. Listen, I'll try him now and let you know what happens, all right?"

He hung up slowly, looking over at Cory. "Well, I *thought* I could ignore Sportsfix this evening, but I guess I can't."

"Someone checking up on you?" she asked lightly.

"My agent. She's been involved in this from the beginning, and right now she's trying to draw up a final budget. The problem is, she can't do that until she has salary figures, and to get those—" he spread his hands wide in an apologetic gesture "—I really do need to call this guy in California, Cory. But I promise I won't be long."

"Sure, Buck. I understand."

He kept looking at her for a few seconds, as if trying to decide whether to take her at her word, and then he turned back to the telephone and dialed a long-distance number. Cory faced the crackling warmth of the fire again and tried to put her thoughts in order while she half listened to Buck speaking.

She heard the growing enthusiasm in his voice as he reached the doctor he was trying to hire. Buck was a dynamo, no doubt about that, and she remembered all too well his unwillingness to give up even a part of the life he'd chosen for himself ten years ago. Would he be that completely immersed in Sportsfix? From the sound of his voice now, she was afraid he would.

She looked into the dancing flames in the fireplace and tried to picture what kind of a life they could have together if she gave in to Buck's urgings now. Buck would be traveling constantly, she knew. He was the kind of man who had to oversee everything himself. And it was entirely possible that he was right. Sportsfix might really be in the vanguard of an expanding new field of medicine. In that case, if the business took off, he would be busier than ever.

And what about her? She knew Buck cared for her. It was impossible to doubt it when he looked at her with that hunger in his eyes. And their attraction for each other was a powerful argument for their being together. But she just couldn't picture herself working at some routine job and waiting for Buck to dash in and out of her life like some unpredictable comet. She wanted more than that from him—much more.

By the time he'd finished his call, she felt she'd cleared up some of the confusion she'd been feeling, and was ready to tell him so. But he immediately dialed another number, saying over his shoulder, "Sorry, but I promised Elaine I'd call her back. I won't be long."

The call dragged on, though, and Cory heard him becoming more and more embroiled in details of hiring staff and drawing up budgets. The longer she waited, the more she wondered if she was crazy to sit here listening to the proof that Buck still wasn't ready to make the compromise she was so sure they needed. After twenty-five minutes of being a reluctant eavesdropper, she stood up and wandered toward the door, thinking that perhaps it was time to put her coat on and leave. She could call a cab from the hotel office and do the rest of her thinking about all of this at home.

"Just a minute, Elaine," she heard Buck say behind her. She turned to see him putting his hand over the mouthpiece of the phone. "I'm almost done, really," he told her. "Don't you dare walk out on me."

"It's getting late, Buck," she said, "and I have to work tomorrow."

"I'll just be two more minutes," he assured her. "And I've just had a great idea. I want to talk to you about it."

This time he was as brief as he'd promised. She heard him asking his agent to keep a couple of staff positions open, at least until the end of the week, and then he said good-night and hung up the phone.

"I really didn't mean to take so long," he apologized. "But in a way I'm glad I did. Come back over here and sit down, and let me tell you what I just thought of."

He motioned her back to the sofa, and slowly she returned to it, sitting next to him but keeping her distance slightly. She didn't want her judgment being clouded by his nearness yet again this evening.

In fact, Buck didn't seem to be thinking about getting closer to her. He was speaking animatedly, leaning forward with his elbows on his knees.

"Elaine keeps after me to hire someone as a consulting nutritionist for Sportsfix," he said. "She says the more people she talks to, the more she's convinced it's something we need to have. I've been stalling on it up to now, because I didn't think it was really important. But even this guy in California asked me if we had a staff nutritionist, so I guess it's something we really do need."

Cory had no idea where he was headed, so she sat listening without speaking. She could tell how completely he was absorbed in this new project of his, just from the sparkle in his dark eyes.

"So here's my idea," he went on. "You're at loose ends at the moment, right? And I can't imagine you want to make a career out of being a dentist's receptionist. So why don't you take a job for Sportsfix, as our resident nutritionist? The pay would be good—we're offering top dollar to all our staff—and you could move to New York again."

He got to his feet, and once again she was reminded of a spring uncoiling. She stood up, too, but before she could interject the protest that had formed on her lips, he went on, "I don't know why I didn't think of it before. It could solve all our problems—you know, living in two different places and wanting to do two separate things. This way we'd be doing the same thing and living in the same place. Hell, we could even travel together—"

She had to stop him before he got so wound up he offered her a contract right there on the spot. "Slow down, Buck," she said. The hard edge in her voice managed to stem the flow of words.

"Of course, I wouldn't expect you to say yes right away," he said, after a moment's pause. "Elaine doesn't have to have a final budget until the end of the week. That gives you a few days, and—"

"What makes you think I'm going to say yes?" she demanded. "You're assuming things again, just like you did with *Five by Ten*. Just because you think something is a good idea, Buck, doesn't mean the whole world agrees with you."

He turned to her, frowning. "But this is a great idea," he argued. "You want to go back to working with food, don't you?"

"Being a chef is completely different from being a nutritionist," she told him. "We're talking about two separate fields."

"Food is food," he insisted stubbornly.

"That's like saying sports are sports," she said. "That doesn't mean a hockey player can switch to baseball, just because he's an athlete."

"Is that your only objection to the idea?"

Cory took a deep breath. "No," she said. "In fact, that's only a very minor part of it. Why can't you seem to understand, Buck, that you're still asking me to mold myself to your life? I just can't do that. If we're going to be together, it has to be on equal terms. And for me to be your employee, fitting myself to your business and your schedule, would be the worst kind of one-sidedness."

She realized she was bracing herself physically, as if she needed the reinforcement for the flood of argument she expected from him. When he remained silent, she made herself relax slowly, letting the tension ease from her muscles.

What was he thinking, behind those lowered brows? She wished she could know for certain, but instead she waited quietly, watching him as he took two long steps away from the fire, then three shorter steps back again.

"I'm doing it again, aren't I?" he asked finally.

That conciliatory, half-joking tone of voice was the last thing she expected from him. She let out her breath, feeling oddly drained. She was worn out from pursuing this problem around and around in a circle.

"Yes, you are," she said, with heartfelt sincerity. "And I'm just worried that you always will."

This time the smile in his eyes turned into a self-deprecating chuckle. "Pushiest son of a gun in the National Hockey League, that's me," he said. "It's funny. Until just this moment, I always thought it was my biggest asset."

"In some ways, it's an asset," she said. "But sometimes it gets in your way."

"I guess it's been getting in my way ever since I've known you, hasn't it?"

She nodded, hoping against hope that some of what she'd said tonight—and ten years ago, for that matter—might finally be getting through to him.

"I've been pretty stubborn," he admitted. But then he added, "And so, for that matter, have you. I wasn't the only one insisting that my career should come first, when we were twenty."

"No," she acknowledged. "I realize that."

He shoved his hands deep into his pockets and glowered at the floor. Cory loved the way his thick hair fell over his forehead, and she had to force herself to keep concentrating on their words, rather than on memories of how touching him had sent a charge throughout her.

Suddenly he gave a short laugh. It didn't sound very amused. "Well, hell," he said, looking up at her. "Maybe we really *are* in the same bind we were ten years ago."

Cory raised her hands to the ceiling. "Hallelujah," she said. "At least we're finally arguing about the same thing."

"That's pretty cold comfort." Buck paced to the bed and back again. "If we still can't work it out—"

He bit off the words, sounding angry all of a sudden. "There's got to be a way," he muttered. "I want you too much to give up now."

"It may be that we just have to wait," she said. "Maybe I was wrong to insist that we have to find an answer right now. Things are bound to change in my life, one way or the other, and then we'll know what we're dealing with. If we're just patient—"

"Patient!" He spat the word out like an expletive. Then, without warning, he took hold of her, pinning her forcefully against him. "How can I be patient, when you make me feel this way?"

And instantly she was drawn back into all the turmoil of feeling that he stirred up in her. When she felt the turbulent pounding of his heart and his unmistakable longing for her the moment her body was molded to his, it became impossible to keep hold of her nice, clear logic. She wrapped her arms around his broad shoulders, still peripherally aware of the fact that passion didn't solve a single thing between them. And logic, she knew just as surely, didn't stand a chance against a passion like this.

His kiss was almost fierce, demanding a response from her. He wasn't giving her choices this time, she thought hazily. She tried halfheartedly to tell him she resented his roughness, but the drugging warmth of his mouth against hers was too distracting. She answered his kisses, clinging to him with convulsive strength.

He tore his lips from hers long enough to bend slightly and slide one strong arm behind her knees. Then he picked her up and strode with her to the big bed. She'd never had the literal sensation of being swept off her feet before, but now, as he stretched himself full-length beside her and covered her lips with his once again, she felt herself being caught in an undertow.

"Cory, do you know it's made me crazy for years, thinking of making love with you?" His voice was ragged, dragged out of him as though these were things he'd promised himself never to tell. "Whole nights I've laid awake, imagining it. I even—" He gave a harsh little laugh, and then forced himself on. "I think I even married another woman because being so lonely for you was driving me out of my mind."

He kissed her neck, her collarbone, the soft base of her ear. Cory was throbbing from head to foot now. Arms like steel pinned her to the bed, and he murmured, "If we made love, Cory, you know you'd have to admit we're right together. What's the use of pretending we're not?"

Cory closed her eyes, feeling as though someone was stirring her emotions into a whirlpool inside her. She could only catch fragments of things as they swept past her—desire for Buck, regret for the past, a mingled hope and fear for the future. She shut her eyes even more tightly, and one thought emerged, strong enough for her to grasp hold of.

"Buck," she said softly, putting her hand across his lips to force him to let her speak, "there's one thing I know for sure. If we made love now, and then we ended up going our separate ways again—" She faltered a little over the words, suddenly feeling all the pain another breakup would cause. "I don't know if I could stand it," she finished lamely. "I'd rather not take the chance."

She heard him groan, and the vibration of his mouth against the palm of her hand nearly undid her resolve. His whole body was pressed erotically against her, creating a hunger more all-embracing than anything she'd ever imagined. It was so tempting to say yes to the moment, to experience at least once the release she'd been seeking in Buck's arms for so long.

But the memory of how she'd felt after losing him before kept intruding. She pushed her hands against his hard chest, and felt him finally give way. Maybe he, too, was realizing that this was just too soon, no matter how much both of them wanted it.

"I'm sorry, Buck." Cory sat up, smoothing back her hair.

"I'm sorry, too." He stayed leaning on one elbow, a shadow of frustrated desire on his handsome face. "I was trying to push you again, Cory. I guess old habits really do die hard."

Maybe old love affairs do, too, she thought unhappily. She wished she knew whether it really might be possible for them to fit their lives together, or whether this whole encounter was just the last gasp of an affair that should have been over ten years ago.

Lacking a crystal ball, she'd just have to wait and see. And for the moment, that was going to be easier to do away from Buck Daly's unsettling presence.

"I really should go, Buck," she said, standing up.

"Not for good, I hope." Beneath his joking tone she heard an undercurrent of seriousness.

"No, of course not. But I need to think things over— alone."

He stood, too. His hair was tousled, and he ran a hand through it. "I understand," he said. "Let me get my keys, and I'll drive you home."

"I'd rather take a cab," she said quickly. "It's not that far."

"Are you sure?"

This was a switch, she thought. He hadn't even argued with her. Maybe she really *had* gotten through this time.

"Quite sure. I'll get the front desk to call me one."

They said good-night almost casually, like two old friends who'd gotten together after not seeing each other for a while. Cory still felt a flash of longing when Buck kissed her gently, but both of them seemed aware of a kind of truce between them, a breathing space, while they figured out where they were headed next.

"I'm determined to hit every interesting restaurant in Keene while I have a competent guide," he told her, walking with her to the door. "Can we meet for dinner tomorrow night?"

"Sure," she said. "Call me tomorrow at the office, and we can set a time."

Compared with the lovemaking they'd been on the verge of, the idea of another polite meal in a restaurant seemed pretty sedate. But it was better this way, Cory told herself, stepping out into the chilly night air and waving goodbye to Buck. She kept telling herself the same thing all the way home in the cab, because it was easier than remembering the look in his eyes as he'd watched her go.

Cold comfort, indeed, she thought.

Seven

Usually Cory didn't feel so tired by the end of the week. Her job wasn't that demanding, and compared to the fourteen-hour days she'd once put in at Horn of Plenty, working nine to five still felt almost like a vacation. But this week, by five o'clock on Friday she was worn out.

She knew it was partly due to the couple of late nights she'd spent with Buck. They'd had dinner out twice, and both times the encounters had turned into long talks over coffee and dessert, as they'd touched on what had seemed like every subject *but* their future together. Cory was grateful for the neutrality of those evenings. It made it much easier to consider what she should do next.

By Friday she'd come to a tentative conclusion. Tired as she was, she scheduled an appointment with a real estate agent she'd talked to earlier in the week, and immediately after leaving work at five, she drove to the piece of property she'd been looking at casually for the past few weeks.

The place would be ideal for a small restaurant, she thought, as she pulled up in front of it. The open space was just the right size for a dining room, and there was ample room for a kitchen in the back. There was plenty of parking, and the location was right. She sighed as she followed the agent and listened to him pointing out the building's advantages, and finally she shook his hand, telling him she was still in the preliminary stages and that she'd get back to him.

Who am I kidding? she asked herself, as she got back into her car and drove home. *I'm nowhere even near the preliminary stages.* But at least she'd taken a step, even a tentative one, toward rebuilding her career, and that was something. Something she owed to Buck, she knew.

Traffic was fairly heavy, and she'd been surrounded by cars until she'd pulled onto her own quiet street. Only then did she notice the dark green car behind her. A careful look in her rearview mirror confirmed her suspicions that Buck was driving it, and she frowned as she pulled into her usual parking space. How long had he been tailing her?

He pulled in right behind her and met her as she opened her car door, answering her unspoken question with a cheery, "Been looking at restaurant properties, have you?"

"How on earth did you know that? Have you been following me?"

"Well, sort of." His grin was as boyish as ever.

"Sort of, nothing. You must have been behind me for ages, if you know where I've been."

"I was going to meet you after work, but you ran out of there so fast I almost missed you. So I followed you. Figured you were going home, not out gallivanting. Looks like a nice piece of property you were scouting out."

He was still following her, right on her heels as she headed for her front door. "Are you seriously looking at it?"

She turned on the top step to look down at him. "How can I look seriously when my chances of getting any financial backing are practically nil?" she asked him. "I was just batting the idea around in my head, that's all."

"Well, even that's an improvement, Cory. Are you going to invite me in?"

Cory thought about it. Would it be wise now to invite him in?

"Strictly a social call," he added, noticing her hesitation.

"All right, then. Come on up."

Cory led the way up the staircase, kicking off her winter boots on the mat at her door. "Just let me get my slippers," she said, as she hung up their two coats on the rack.

Buck remained standing in her tastefully decorated living room as Cory disappeared into the bedroom. It was still a major effort for him not to drag her into his arms every time they met, and the thought of standing here while she was in her bedroom was a subtle torture for him.

But he recognized that he'd made a mistake on Tuesday night, in trying to force her to open up to him. She obviously still needed more time to think things over, and the fact that she'd actually gone looking at restaurant property today proved that this new arrangement was working. It was damned hard, though, Buck thought, resolutely standing his ground and not heading down the hall to where he could hear a soft opening and closing of closet doors.

"That's better," she said, returning to the living room. "Now, what's your social call about?"

"Two things. First of all, can you stand to have dinner with me again tonight?"

"Sure. We still haven't gone to the Copper Cauldron."

"I thought you said it was too trendy."

"Well, it is, but their seafood is fantastic on Fridays. I haven't had a decent lobster bisque in ages."

"All right, the Copper Cauldron it is. And the other thing—" Buck cleared his throat. He hoped he could bring this up in a way that wouldn't ruin the easy mood between them just now. "The other thing has to do with Theodore."

"Oh?" She arched one eyebrow delicately. He'd never been able to figure out how she did that and still managed to look beautiful.

"Yes. He called me last night. Actually, he's called me a couple of times this week."

"You never mentioned it." She seated herself in a chair, the full skirt of her tan shirtwaist dress swirling around her knees like a cape. She wore her hair up today in an elegant twist, and it made Buck's fingers itch to let down those satiny dark blond tresses and feel his fingers running through them.

He cleared his throat again. "I didn't think it was worth going into," he said. "But now I think it is, because Theodore's coming up to his deadline for getting this show together, and he's putting a lot of pressure on me to get you to agree to it."

"What kind of pressure?"

"You know Theodore. He just keeps working away at something until he gets what he wants."

"Sounds like another person I know," she responded lightly.

"I'm doing better, aren't I?" Buck smiled, although he couldn't tell, from her level aquamarine gaze, whether she really believed him or not. For all he knew, she still suspected his whole visit here had to do with *Five by Ten*.

He was momentarily heartened when she said, "You're right. I wasn't being quite fair." But then she added, almost immediately, "What about *Five by Ten*? That's just as important to you as ever, isn't it?"

"In one way. In another, it barely matters now."

She frowned and seemed on the point of asking him to explain himself when the doorbell rang. Buck sighed, and as Cory stood up to answer the insistent chiming, he took her by the shoulders and said hastily, "I just wanted to warn you, Cory. Theodore said something crazy about coming up here himself to convince you, if you wouldn't listen to me. I don't know whether he meant it or not, but if that's him..."

The sudden wariness in her eyes kept him from completing the sentence. "If that's Theodore, he's going to find out the same thing I've been telling you for over a week," she said. "And that's that I refuse to be pressured into doing something."

Buck stood silently at the top of the stairs while she answered the door, and his fervent hope that the visitor should be something innocuous like a Girl Guide cookie seller vanished when he heard the first robust words from the man on the step.

"Cory, my dear! More beautiful than ever."

That was Theodore Aiken, all right. And loading on the charm, Buck thought. He listened hard to hear what Cory's response would be. He knew she'd always been fond of the outgoing director.

"Well, Theodore." Her voice was noncommittal. "I heard you might be in the neighborhood."

"Did you? Then this isn't such a surprise. Well, it's wonderful to see you, surprise or not. Aren't you going to invite me in?"

Buck smiled involuntarily. Cory seemed to be besieged this evening with men on her doorstep, asking whether she was going to invite them in. From the smile in her voice when she answered, she was amused by the same thought. "Sure," she said. "Come in and join the party." And then, once again, she led the way upstairs. He saw a slightly mutinous look in her eye when she met his gaze.

The stocky director wasn't much taller than Cory's five-foot-six, Buck thought, but Theodore had a way of filling a room, taking center stage wherever he was. He immediately took over the situation now, greeting Buck effusively and complimenting Cory on everything from her hair to the stylish prints on her living room wall.

"Thanks, Theodore," she said, and Buck caught the dryness in her tone. "The pictures originally hung in my restaurant. That's kaput now, as I guess you've heard."

"I have. And very sorry to hear it, too. But listen—I'm starved, haven't eaten since breakfast. Let's not talk about anything at all until we've had something to eat, all right? My treat. I'm sure Cory knows all the good places to eat in Keene."

Buck glanced at Cory, wishing he knew what she was thinking. She was being friendly enough to Theodore, but was she resenting his invasion as she'd resented Buck's a week ago? Theodore's sense of timing couldn't have been worse, he thought ruefully. By barging in right now, the director could very well throw a wrench into the fragile beginnings of the new relationship Cory and Buck were building.

Well, she wasn't giving any hint of what she was feeling as she said, "We were just getting ready to go out to dinner ourselves. Why don't you join us?"

Theodore pronounced that that would be delightful, and even refused to take his coat off and have a drink first. "I do need to make one quick phone call, and then I'll be ready. By the way, where were you planning to go for dinner?''

"It's a place called the Copper Cauldron," Cory told him. "Their seafood is terrific on Fridays." She pointed out the kitchen wall phone and pulled the louvered door closed behind her to give Theodore some privacy. His call was as quick as he promised, and he soon reemerged, declaring himself ready to eat a shark.

Buck thought suspiciously that Theodore's hurry probably had less to do with hunger than with his plan for changing Cory's mind as quickly as possible. But he didn't say anything about it as the three of them drove in Buck's car to the Copper Cauldron.

The restaurant was packed, but they managed to get a table after only a few minutes' wait. Unfortunately, the table was in the middle of the bustling floor area, instead of in one of the raised alcoves all around the edge, as Cory had hoped. "This can be a little like eating in a fishbowl," she commented, trying to smile about it as they took their seats. Buck didn't seem to mind the central location, she noticed, and Theodore was positively reveling in being right in the middle of things. In some ways, she reflected, he was as much of an attention-monger as Heck James.

"You should definitely try the lobster bisque," she said, hoping to keep the conversation to neutral subjects for a while, at least. "And the shrimp étouffé is excellent, too."

"Anything you recommend is fine by me," Theodore said expansively. But once they'd ordered, he dropped his pretense of just having dropped in for a visit, and leaned his elbows on the edge of the table, looking seriously across to Cory.

"I'm very sorry to hear Buck hasn't been able to convince you to do the show, Cory," he said. "I've been hoping we could all work together again before long."

"Hey, Theodore," Buck intervened. "Why don't we leave the business talk till after dinner, at least?"

"After dinner I've got to get back in my car and drive all the way home to New York," Theodore said, and they both caught a glimpse of the iron will they remembered was just beneath that smiling surface. "I haven't got much time to say what I want to say."

"I'm sorry, too, Theodore," Cory cut in, answering Theodore's original statement, "but surely Buck had explained to you why I'm hesitating over being on *Five by Ten*."

"He said something about you not wanting to expose yourself to any more unfavorable publicity. Now, I can understand that, but what *you* don't seem to understand, Cory, is how many people out there are dying to see another episode of the show. These people are big fans of yours, Cory. They remember when you were just a shy little ten-year-old with braids, and they're certainly not going to believe a vague rumor that's never been substantiated."

"It's a lot more than a vague rumor, Theodore. Eight people nearly died in my restaurant."

"Because someone poisoned them, yes. But it makes no sense that you would have done a thing like that."

"I hired the person who did," she said tightly. "In the eyes of the law, that may make me responsible for what happened."

"That's ridiculous." Theodore had always had a way of making pronouncements, Cory remembered. "And now, here are our appetizers. Let's take Buck's advice and not talk business while we eat."

The lobster bisque was as good as Cory remembered it. She ate silently, trying to analyze the soup's ingredients as a way of distracting herself from Theodore's insistent probing. A touch of tarragon, she thought, and a little sherry, perhaps. She was concentrating hard on the flavors when Buck's low voice cut into her thoughts.

"Don't look now," he was saying to her, "but Heck James just walked in."

Cory put down her spoon. That was all she needed tonight. "I should have remembered Heck thinks this is the best place in town to see and be seen," she said. "Especially on a Friday night when things are busiest."

Theodore was looking from one to the other of them, clearly curious, and Cory explained, "Heck is the man in the loud plaid jacket by the door. He's the one who backed my restaurant originally, but we've had a, well, a falling out, and I'm not crazy about running into him."

"He seems to be alone," Buck said. "If we're in luck, he'll be meeting someone."

They weren't in luck. Heck's watchful small eyes were scanning the busy restaurant, and before long they'd lighted on the table where Cory, Buck and Theodore sat. He waved off the waiter who was handing him a menu, and headed for the middle of the floor area.

"Cory, nice to see you," he said, waving a fleshy hand. "Buck, good to run into you again. Didn't realize you were still in Keene."

"Well, I just can't get enough of the peace and quiet around here," Buck said pointedly, but this time his hint fell on deaf ears.

Worse yet, to Cory's consternation, Theodore was standing up and introducing himself, putting out a welcoming hand. "Mr. James," he said, with his cheeriest smile. "You don't likely remember me. I'm Theodore

Aiken. I believe we met years ago on the set of *Five by Ten*
when you came down to see a taping.''

Heck's eyes were wider than Cory had seen them in a
long time. Theodore was playing the humble celebrity, she
thought, and Heck was lapping it up.

''Of course,'' Heck said, pumping Theodore's hand and
taking a seat in the extra chair Theodore pulled out for him.
''Well, you're probably the last person I expected to see in
our little town. You folks must be having a good old reunion here.''

''Well, that's the idea,'' Theodore said smoothly, as
though responding to a cue card, and Cory kicked herself
inwardly for getting drawn into any of this. She glanced
angrily across the table at Buck, and saw that he, too, was
realizing what Theodore's game was. The wily director was
enlisting an ally, and Cory didn't like it.

''Aren't you meeting someone here, Heck?'' she asked
him.

''Actually, I'm on my own tonight,'' he replied. ''But
you know how it is in a little place like this one. You're always running into a friend or a neighbor.''

Especially if you worked as hard as Heck did on culti-
vating influential friends and neighbors, she thought,
frustrated at the way Heck and Theodore had gate-crashed
her dinner with Buck. Well, she might as well make the best
of it, she decided. At least the seafood was good enough to
take her mind off Theodore's ploys and Heck's obvious
social climbing.

Buck, too, seemed to have opted to concentrate on his
dinner rather than on socializing. That was all very well
until they'd finished their meal and had ordered coffee.
Then, as Cory and Buck both discovered, there was no polite way to avoid talking about the subject Theodore raised
once again.

"So, Heck," Theodore said, pouring cream into his coffee, "are you still speculating on restaurant properties?"

Heck looked quickly at Cory, and then away again. At least he had the good grace to seem a little embarrassed, she noted with satisfaction.

"Not really," he hedged. "Cory was a special case, you know—a real 'local girl makes good' story. We were all pretty excited when she graduated from that fancy school."

"I thought you were excited because I'd been featured on a national TV show, Heck," she said carefully. She didn't want to argue with the man, but his hypocrisy with Theodore bothered her.

"Well, that, too, of course," he admitted.

Theodore jumped in before Cory could say anything else. "Did you know there's been a proposal to do another episode of *Five by Ten*?" he asked Heck.

"Wouldn't that be something, now?" The businessman looked at Cory again, speculatively this time. "With the same people, you mean?"

"Of course. Naturally, we'd need to get all five of them together again."

"Well, naturally. So *that's* why you're all meeting like this."

"Actually," Cory said clearly, "we're meeting like this because these two have been trying to convince me to do the show, and at this point, I'm not sure if I want to." She didn't know just what Theodore was up to, but she wanted to speak for herself before he manipulated the conversation anymore. She'd remembered Theodore as being a bit autocratic, but she'd never seen him quite this determined to have his own way at any cost.

"That's a shame, Cory," Heck was saying. "That was a good show."

"It was," she agreed. "But it just might have to go on without me."

Theodore turned to face Cory's former backer. "Cory feels that it would be too painful an experience to have to tell the world about her restaurant," he said. "Of course, we can all understand that."

"It's not done yet, Heck." Cory heard her own voice getting a bit brittle. She hated talking about it, even with just a few people around. A quick glance across the table showed her the top of Buck's head; apparently he was absorbed in studying his coffee. So much for support from his corner, she thought. She really was on her own, just as she'd insisted to Buck from the beginning.

"Not done? Oh, you mean that lawsuit. Well, I'm sure they won't find you guilty, Cory."

"What makes you so sure, Heck?" she challenged him. "You didn't even believe in my innocence enough to make me a loan to keep my restaurant going. What makes you think the Supreme Court will have any more sympathy for me?"

Heck colored uncomfortably. Cory refused to feel sorry for him; he'd caused her enough sleepless nights, she thought.

Again Theodore intervened smoothly. "Heck's a businessman," he said reasonably. "He can't afford to back a questionable investment, no matter how much he may trust you personally."

"He backed me before, when I was riding high," Cory said, refusing to give way. Why was Buck so silent? she wondered. He'd hardly said a word since Heck had joined them.

"Exactly. And now that you've had an offer to do *Five by Ten* again, perhaps he'd be willing to reconsider, and fund you again,'' Theodore said. Then he sat back, having dropped his bombshell.

For a moment Cory just looked at him, trying to piece together what was happening here. Was Theodore actually implying that if Cory did her show, Heck would back her in opening a new restaurant? She shifted her gaze to Heck and saw him beaming as if Theodore had just pulled a rabbit out of a hat. Buck must have told the director everything, she realized: Heck's betrayal of her, the lawsuit, everything.

And Theodore had used it to good advantage. Suddenly she saw what was really going on, and it made her so angry that for a moment she knew what it meant to see red. Certainly a scarlet haze obscured her vision for a moment, and when it cleared again, she said in a shaking voice, ''Now I understand. Theodore, I can't believe you set this up.''

''Now, Cory—'' He wasn't denying it, she noticed. He was holding out a placating hand, as though he'd expected everything to be all right now that he'd put his cards on the table.

''You invited Heck here, didn't you? That was the phone call you made from my place. This whole thing was just an act to bribe me into doing your show.''

Theodore's face was serious now, his voice calm. ''Be reasonable, Cory. Buck told me you'd had thoughts of starting another restaurant. Well, *Five by Ten* can be your chance of doing that. Heck is a businessman, not a charitable foundation. He's not going to fund something just out of the goodness of his heart. But if there's favorable publicity in it for him, perhaps you two can work out a deal. Yes, I invited him here. But it's for your own good, can't you see that?''

Cory very gently set down her coffee cup, to keep from giving in to the impulse to slam it against the saucer. Some splintering crockery would have been a very satisfying sound just now. "Thanks for the good intentions, Theodore," she said tightly, "but I don't need the help, all right?"

Heck James jumped in now, too, eager to change Cory's mind. "I've been truly sorry I couldn't help you out when you needed a loan a couple of years ago," he said. "But Theodore's quite right. I can't go around loaning money on a whim. I've got to turn a profit if I'm going to stay in business. But this, now—if your name was well-known again in connection with a popular TV show, that could more than offset the publicity from two years ago."

His wheedling tone of voice made Cory's blood boil. No doubt everything he and Theodore were saying made perfect sense, but it made her feel like a commodity, something to be traded while its value was high.

"Why don't you both just come out and admit that you want to make use of Cory to get something for yourselves?"

Buck's deep voice broke into the conversation with an unexpected force. All three of them looked at him, and he continued, "You just want to get your show made, Theodore. I can understand that—I'd like to see *Five by Ten* air again, too. But I'm not resorting to bribery to achieve it. And you, Mr. James." Cory could hear the dislike in his voice. "Don't you think you're being a bit obvious about all this? If I made a habit of only supporting my friends when they were doing well, I wouldn't be as quick to admit it as you seem to be."

"Now, look here, that's not what I meant," Heck blustered.

"Sure sounded like it from where I sat."

Buck pushed back his chair and stood. "Cory has a perfect right to make up her own mind about doing the show," he said slowly. "And I wouldn't blame her for being a bit leery of taking your money on any terms, Mr. James. An unreliable patron is just as bad as an unreliable investment, isn't it?"

He'd kept his voice low, but there was a barely repressed anger in it that made his words riveting. For Cory, listening to him was like taking a deep breath of fresh spring air after languishing inside all winter. He was saying exactly what she felt, with a calmness and strength she couldn't muster for herself right now. Her anger had made it too difficult to think straight, but Buck was taking up the slack.

Following his lead, she stood, too, and picked up her pocketbook. "I don't think we need to discuss this any further," she said politely. "Thanks for the dinner, Theodore. It was very...enlightening."

And then, as if they'd planned it, she and Buck turned in unison and made for the door. They put their coats on in silence, not looking back to see what Theodore's and Heck's reactions had been. Only when they were outside in the crisp moonlit night did they look at each other, and then without warning, they both started to laugh.

"Buck, thank you," Cory said, smiling widely. "I really owe you one."

He was still smiling himself as he opened the car's passenger door. His words, though, sounded serious. "Believe me, it was my pleasure," he said. "And I figured I owed *you*, after all the badgering I've done."

"I still can't believe Theodore tried something that blatant." The air inside the car was frigid, and Cory's words made white puffs of breath as she spoke.

"I can. He told me when he called today that he had a couple of studio executives really breathing down his neck on this project. If he pulls it off, it'll mean big points for him with the studio. If he can't do it, he'll be in the dog-house.''

"I see. Well, that still doesn't change my point of view."

"Of course not. It *was* a dirty trick."

They didn't speak much on the drive home, except to speculate how Theodore was going to get back to his car—"Heck will drive him," Cory said with certainty. "He loves to drive celebrities''—and whether he would give up and go back to New York as he'd planned. "If he doesn't, pretty soon there may be a whole colony of people taking up temporary residence in Keene for the purpose of getting me to do *Five by Ten*," Cory said.

"There are worse things to do," Buck said lightly, as he pulled onto Cory's street.

To her surprise, he didn't offer to see her to the door this time. Instead, he said, "Theodore isn't the only one who has to be back in New York before long. I've really got to get back, to settle some things about Sportsfix that I can't do on the phone."

"When are you leaving?" The thought of not having Buck around cast a sudden chill on Cory's heart.

"Tomorrow sometime, I'm afraid." He paused, and then added. "Will you be glad to be rid of me?"

"Rid of you!" She shook her head. "Having you around has been, well, in some ways, it's been more fun than I've had in ten years."

"I was hoping to hear you say that. Because it's been a special time for me, too." He leaned toward her a little, and Cory felt herself moving closer to him, wanting to touch and be touched by him.

He kissed her so gently that she almost begged him for more. But she sensed there was something on his mind, and she asked him in a near-whisper what it was.

His voice was like warm velvet in the wintery air. "I'm going to ask you one more time about *Five by Ten*, and I'm willing to take your answer as final," he told her. "Will you or won't you do the show?"

He found himself holding his breath, almost dreading her answer. Theodore's show was far from the main reason he'd stayed around in Keene, he knew, and if Cory said no, his life would hardly come to an end. But the show as his excuse to see her, and the easiest way to keep in contact without putting too many other demands on her right away. If she said no, it might be more difficult for them to keep on building what they'd started. And he hardly dared hope she'd say yes.

She said neither. She only asked, "What time are you leaving?"

"About noon, I think."

She regarded him levelly for a moment. Then she said, "I'll have a final answer for you by then, all right?"

He let out his breath in a faint white cloud. "All right," he said, and kissed her again. "Good night, Cory. Sleep well." She smiled at him as she left the car, and he wondered if she would sleep at all. He certainly didn't imagine he'd be able to.

Eight

The moon was full, and at first Cory thought that was what was keeping her awake. She'd puttered around her place for a couple of hours after Buck had dropped her off, finishing little cleaning jobs she hadn't been able to get to during the week. Usually that was her way of winding down after a hectic day, but tonight she stayed wide-awake, and it seemed like a waste of time to go to bed yet.

At about eleven-thirty she got out a pad of lined paper and pen and sat down at her dining room table. Telling herself this was only a diversion to pass the time, she began drawing up projections of what it would cost her to open a new restaurant. From listing figures, she quickly progressed to sketching floor plans, and pretty soon menus were suggesting themselves to her as well. She became completely absorbed in what she was doing, forgetting she'd started it as a game, and for more than two hours she let herself dream as she'd refused to do for the past two years.

She was astonished to look at her kitchen clock and see that it was approaching 2:00 a.m., and even more astonished that she'd managed to do all of this without remembering that the whole project only existed in her imagination. To bring herself back to earth, she totaled up the costs she'd listed on the first page of her calculations, and the size of the bank loan she'd need to apply for brought her back to earth in a big hurry. Even an imaginary bank officer was never going to go for that one, she thought.

Well, at least it had been fun for a couple of hours. The strange thing was, she still wasn't sleepy. She made a couple of turns around her apartment, willing herself to feel tired, but her brain was still humming with ideas, and foremost among them was that Buck was going away the next day.

That was what was keeping her from sleeping, she admitted finally. He was still here, not far from her, in his rented cabin on the outskirts of Keene. And tomorrow he'd be in New York. She'd paced a couple more times around her living room before she realized that she wasn't going to sleep no matter what she did, and that she'd be crazy to miss this one last opportunity to tell Buck just how she felt about him. Without stopping to let the cool voice of reason interfere, she put on her coat and boots and went down the stairs, car keys in hand.

Just how *did* she feel about Buck? She dared to ask herself the question as she approached the turn for his hotel, and for the first time she admitted to herself that she loved him just as much as she had ten years ago—more, because both of them had grown and matured in the intervening years. True, there were still things keeping them apart. But just for now, in this still, moonlit winter night, the only thing that mattered to Cory was that she loved him.

The lights were still on in his cabin, and her heart started to beat faster at the sight. She parked her car next to his and walked quietly up the path to the cabin. Heart thumping violently by now, she tapped on the door.

It opened a moment later, and the look on Buck's face was midway between desire and disbelief. "Cory..." he breathed. "Did I conjure you up? I've been sitting here fantasizing about you knocking on my door for the past three hours."

"Maybe that was why I couldn't sleep," she smiled. She stepped over the threshold and saw that there was a fire in the fireplace warming the small cabin. "You look like you've been doing the same thing I have."

Neither of them had changed out of the clothes they'd worn to the restaurant, she noted. Although she had let down her hair, she was still wearing her full-skirted tan dress, and Buck had on the white shirt and the trousers from the dark suit. She could see the jacket and tie tossed casually over the back of the sofa.

"And what have you been doing?" There was a dangerous magic in his glittering brown eyes as he closed the door behind her.

"Pacing around and wondering why I couldn't sleep." Cory took in a deep breath, and turned to face him. "And I finally decided why that was."

"Tell me. Maybe we've got the same problem."

"If your problem is the thought of being apart from each other, then we do."

She saw his eyes darken at her words, and sensed the passion in him. Not only had they been thinking the same thoughts, she realized, but they were feeling the same excitement now. It was a heady notion, and she felt a pleasurable trembling begin to fill her limbs as he watched her.

He took a step closer, as though he still couldn't quite believe she'd come. "Oh, God, Cory," was all the answer he got out before he captured her in his arms, pressing his face into her hair. She could feel him drawing in a deep, shuddering breath, and she twined her arms tightly around him, reassuring him that for the moment, there was no need to think of anything but the sheer exhilaration of being together.

Buck lifted his head, studying her face, and then with a faint, almost triumphant smile, he kissed her. Cory couldn't resent the smile; she was feeling some of the same triumph herself as their two bodies fused together, acknowledging the hunger they both felt. Finally, for some reason she didn't bother to define, it was so right to be holding Buck this way, letting go to the unstoppable drive within her.

"You look so lovely," he was murmuring, his lips still grazing hers. "Just like the princess in the fairy tale."

"Maybe it's the full moon," she whispered back, "but I think the spell is finally broken."

She leaned her head back to look at him, and her hair swayed like a satin curtain. Buck took in another long breath, feeling the fire raging in his veins at the sight and smell of her. Touching her was an exquisite agony that he wanted to prolong forever.

He kissed her again, and Cory could feel the way he was forcing himself to move slowly, as though they were embracing each other in an underwater ballet. She sensed him trying to draw out this moment, making it last forever, and she wondered if her own growing desire for him would let her go along. She opened her lips to him, feeling the surge building inside her as their mouths moved together more and more intimately, tongues exploring the warm realms of pleasure and pulses pounding with the realization of where they could take each other.

Buck's strong fingers were tangling themselves in her hair, framing her chin. Suddenly their clothes seemed ridiculously in the way, especially when she ran her own hands through his thick dark hair and felt the heat of his skin under her fingertips. She wanted desperately to touch all of him and to see that glorious body of his. From the barely repressed moan she heard in the back of his throat, she knew he was picturing the same thing.

He finally raised his head, and his voice was low and ragged as he told her, "The thing that keeps me awake nights is thinking about undressing you, feeling all of your skin like silk under my fingers." He traced a line from her lips to the high collar of her dress, and Cory's imagination took over from there. She knew precisely how knowing he would be, and it made him impossible to resist.

His words intoxicated her, calling up images that turned her bones to water. "And to think I once told you words weren't your strong point," she whispered.

"I'm still pretty good on action, too," he assured her, his mouth tilting briefly into that impossibly youthful smile.

"Are you?" Her eyes were fastened to his now, asking him for everything he could give her. "Show me, Buck."

Her breathless order seemed to catapult him into a new realm of need for her. Without pausing, he flicked open the buttons at the front of her dress and kissed the spot where her pulse throbbed at the base of her neck. Then he raised his hands, pushing the dress back from her shoulders. She felt the fabric slide against her arms, and undid the belt herself, letting the whole dress fall to the floor at her feet.

Her head fell back in utter pleasure as Buck ran his hands over the satin slip that covered her. His fingers seemed to know her intimately already, as they sought out her breasts and caressed the tightly contracted nipples. Cory was floating now, completely abandoned to the heat that seemed to engulf her from inside and out.

His motions were deliberate, almost reverent as he pushed the straps of her slip from her shoulders and watched the satiny garment fall to the floor. The best efforts of Cory's imagination hadn't been able to prepare her for the magical reality of his hands against her bare skin. She trembled, barely aware of shedding the panty hose that were the only remaining barrier between her flesh and Buck's fingers.

Still moving slowly, as though he wanted to prolong this pleasure, he lowered himself to his knees on the soft carpet. Cory felt his warm breath and the searching hunger of his kisses against her skin, and moaned out loud as his hands roved over her body, never stopping at one place quite long enough to satisfy the demands his caresses were creating.

She was now throbbing in every part of her body. She'd always tried so hard to control the passion that Buck Daly brought out in her, and now that she had finally given in, it coursed through her with a sweet, consuming need that left her gasping.

She could feel his strong frame shudder as he ran his fingers lightly over her unfettered breasts. "I didn't think anything could be more beautiful than the way I imagined you," he said hoarsely. "But you're even lovelier than I dreamed."

Then his mouth was exploring her soft skin, creating ripples that ran all the way through her. Her nerves were on fire, supercharged by the knowing warmth of his mouth and the way he surrounded her breasts and aroused them with his tongue. How could he know so precisely what would make her feel this way? Cory swayed in his grasp, lost in the sensations he was arousing in her.

She felt no shyness with him, only desire. How could a woman feel shy when she was being so openly adored? Cory reveled in every kiss he placed on her skin, feeling a whole new kind of awareness spring into life at every spot he touched.

"Buck, this is crazy," she managed to say, as she twirled her fingers in his thick hair and glanced down at him with languid, half-open eyes. "You haven't even taken your shirt off, in case you'd forgotten."

Her words seemed to surprise him. He looked up at her with a lopsided smile. "I *had* forgotten," he said, and straightened. He seemed to have a hard time tearing himself away from the softness of her body, but once he finally managed, he shed his clothes in a matter of seconds.

Then he recaptured her in his arms, and the sight and feel of him took Cory's growing desire into a whole new dimension. He looked even stronger without his clothes, and she couldn't resist running her hands over the muscles in his shoulders and chest.

Since adolescence she'd been picturing him unclothed, with a half-guilty pleasure she'd never been able to resist. His confident, spring-loaded gait...the masterful way he moved on the ice...everything about him had fired her imagination even before she'd dreamed of falling in love with him. Now, finally, those fantasies had become real, and with a kind of joyful pleasure she hadn't known she could feel, she explored the roundness of his shoulders, the taut smooth muscles of his upper arms, the flat plane of his stomach and the hard wall of his chest, like living granite.

"Oh, God," she heard him groan. "You can do that all day, as far as I'm concerned."

Cory doubted it. The need she was feeling was escalating too fast, and the more she let her hands discover the strength of his body, the more inescapably she thought of how their two bodies would merge together completely.

She let him steer her toward the big bed, and when they had stretched out together on the soft wool bedspread, the feeling of touching him along the whole length of his body was more exciting than Cory could have imagined. Her skin felt achingly alive wherever it met his, and when he half turned to pin her under him, and the powerful muscles of his thigh pushed against her hip, she felt the strength of his arousal with an almost painful intensity. Nothing in her modest experience of lovemaking could compare with the things Buck was making her feel, just by lying next to her.

Being still was not enough, for either of them. Cory wrapped her legs seductively around his, bringing him closer to her, and at the same time he let his hands travel over all of her body, seeking out corners of her that Cory had never dreamed could be so responsive.

He spent a long time tracing the line of her thigh, starting at the back of her knee and moving upward, stopping just short of the places that were clamoring for his touch. Again and again he followed that long, smooth line, moving inward all the time, until Cory heard her own voice begging for more.

Still he made her wait, building up her response to a fever pitch. He ran his hand over her stomach, just as far as the first curling hairs his fingers encountered, and then back up again to her breasts. Cory was half-delirious with anticipation, and her own hunger made her bolder than she'd ever been with a man.

With each movement he made, she could see the strength of his muscles moving beneath his skin. Every part of him was hard, powerful from years of training himself to move quickly and surely. His shoulders, when she touched them, make her think of the perfection of a marble statue come to living, breathing life. And the more she let her hands and mouth explore him, the more she knew she was arousing him, maddening him just as surely as he was maddening her.

Finally neither of them could stand it any longer. Buck's eyes were dark with passion, his breathing deep and unsteady, as he moved above her. Cory was trembling in every limb, wanting him, and when he slid inside her with one long, sure movement, she knew this was what had been beckoning to her from Buck's dark eyes for the past ten years.

For an instant she thought the feeling of him inside her was all she could ever want or need. Then, suddenly, it *wasn't* enough. She had to move with him to a point in the shimmering distance that seemed to be beckoning to her, lighting up the darkness behind her closed eyes. She raised herself to meet him, matching every thrust and urging on the rhythm that was building up in her.

"Oh, God, Cory..."

The light behind her eyes was becoming brighter. She heard Buck's voice calling her name, like an invitation to quicken her movements. Their bodies were completely united now, moving with one thought to that same glowing place.

They reached it suddenly, with no warning, and the explosion of light in Cory's head was like a physical shock. For a long moment it blinded her, making space and time into meaningless things, and then, slowly, it diffused itself into random spots of brilliance, shooting stars, and the hazy image of Buck's face changed and torn by the same indescribable passion.

As she opened her eyes more fully, his face came into focus, and she could see in his eyes the wonder of what they'd just shared. His lips parted, as though he was going to speak, and then he seemed to change his mind.

Cory agreed. There were no words for what they needed to say. She held him closely as he moved to lie beside her on the bed, and by the time he reached down to pull the spare blanket over them, she was already drifting into a pleasurable half sleep. Reality had its pleasures, too, but for the moment, Cory chose to stay in that world of dream and desire that Buck had opened up for her.

She slept without dreaming until morning. When she finally opened her eyes, the fire in the grate was out, and Buck was rubbing his eyes as though he, too, had just surfaced from sleep.

"What time is it?" she asked, without really caring.

"Late," he said, rolling over to look at his bedside clock. "It's almost nine."

She remembered, with an unpleasant little chill, that he was supposed to leave today. "You said you were checking out around noon, didn't you?" she asked carefully.

His face told her he wasn't looking forward to it any more than she was. "I'm afraid so," he said. "I really do have to be back in New York tonight."

She snuggled against him, deciding to deny reality for the time being. But before long it intruded again, and she recalled that the ostensible reason she'd come to Buck's cabin last night was to talk about *Five by Ten*.

"Remember I told you I'd have an answer about the show by this morning?" she asked him.

"Mmm?" For the first time, Buck seemed to have no interest at all in the television show. He was holding her to him in a way that was exciting both of them again, and

Cory knew that if they were going to talk things over, they couldn't be quite this close to each other. Reluctantly she moved away, rolling over so she was facing him.

"I'm serious, Buck," she said, softening her words by the loving way she reached out to smooth the dark hair that had become tousled by sleep and passion.

He took her hand, kissed the palm sensuously, and said, "All right, shoot. I'm ready for anything."

"Are you ready to hear me agree to do the show?"

He looked startled, and she knew she'd caught him off guard. "Are you serious?"

"I already said I was."

"But Cory, I— What changed your mind?"

She shrugged, pulling the covers a little higher on her shoulder. The air in the cabin was chillier since the fire had died, and the warmth of being in this big bed next to Buck's body was pure heaven.

"A lot of things, I guess," she said. She'd been trying to explain this to herself, and she still wasn't sure she understood her own change of mind.

"Such as . . ."

"Such as the way you stood up for me with Theodore and Heck last night. You wouldn't have done that if all you wanted was the publicity *Five by Ten* can give you."

"You're right about that. It made my blood boil, seeing those two try to buy your cooperation that way."

"Well, the things you said to them made me feel that you and I are on the same side in this, instead of being adversaries. It was a new feeling for me."

She looked up at him, wondering if he'd understand. He was nodding, assuring her he did.

"We've always seemed to be fighting about something up to now, haven't we?" he asked softly.

"We sure have."

"Do you think we're past all that now?"

"I don't know." She looked back down at the white sheets, tracing an invisible pattern with her fingernail. "There are still a lot of things we have to deal with."

"Such as your lawsuit and your career," he supplied.

"And *your* career," she reminded him. "I have to have a life of my own. And speaking of that—" she took in a deep breath, feeling as though she was baring her soul "—I spent the time when I wasn't pacing last night drawing up some crazy plans for a new restaurant. And I know it may never happen, but—"

She'd been going to explain that at least she felt she was looking forward now, instead of being bogged down in her present situation, but Buck didn't let her get that far. He sat up suddenly, dragging the covers with him.

"Cory, that's great! Are you thinking of here in Keene or somewhere else?"

"I haven't said I'm really thinking of anywhere yet, Buck. Just hold on a minute."

She should have remembered he was incapable of holding on, once a new enthusiasm had seized him. She sighed and slid back under the covers as he bolted out of bed, wrapping himself in a burgundy-colored robe.

"I knew you'd get back in the saddle sooner or later," he was saying, "and I've been thinking about how to do it. Look, I know you don't like Heck James, but he *is* offering you a loan, and that could be your ticket."

Cory's warm, euphoric mood was disappearing fast. "I wouldn't take a penny of Heck's money," she said crisply. "He let me down once, and I'm not giving him the chance to do it again."

"Wait, there's more. You take Heck's loan, see, and open a restaurant. And then you and I set up a corporation, to cover your business and mine, so if you have lean times again, there'll be something to cushion you, and you won't have to be dependent on Heck.''

"I'll just be dependent on Sportsfix then, won't I?"

"Sure, but where's the harm in that?"

"What if the clinics don't turn a profit? And anyway, Buck, who's going to run this corporation? It's not simply a matter of making up an organization on paper, you know."

"I know. I'll run it."

"*And* manage Sportsfix? *And* have any time for yourself? Doesn't sound very likely to me."

She still couldn't state baldly her fears that Buck was always going to be dashing impetuously off in a zillion directions, leaving no time for the home life that was necessary to a lasting relationship. Instead, she said, "Thanks for thinking of all this, Buck, but I'm afraid you're missing the point again. Rebuilding my career is up to me and me alone. It's *us* that you should be worrying about."

She could see him trying to come to a halt, shifting gears as he took in what she was saying. "Are you worried about us?" he demanded, coming back to sit on the bed beside her.

"In some ways, yes."

"In some ways." He leaned over as he echoed her words, sliding one strong hand under the sheet. The magic of his touch reminded her instantly of all the ways she *wasn't* worried about.

"We can talk about it some more later," she murmured. "When I come to New York."

"Sounds good to me." In one movement he shed his robe and moved back under the covers with her, and once they'd joined the lengths of their two bodies under the smooth sheets, Cory forgot all about the misgivings she still hadn't been able to overcome. She forgot, too, how chilly she'd found the air in the cabin. There was another fire now, she thought, as Buck kissed her slowly, almost lazily. The fire was inside her and it was burning bright.

Nine

——

Annie, I can't afford a new suit."

"How can you resist this one? It would be perfect for you."

The two women were walking back to work after a quick get-together over lunch, and they had paused in front of a display of new spring suits in the window of a women's store.

"I've got that navy blue suit I bought two years ago for my court appearance," Cory protested.

"You want to be reminded of going to court? Forget it. Anyway, that suit won't go with Buck's scarf."

In a weak moment, Cory had told her friend about Buck's birthday present, the beautiful scarf that was still lying unworn in its box. Annie was quite right in saying the ivory wool suit in the store window would go perfectly with the scarf's muted colors.

"Seems a little extravagant, buying a whole suit to go with a scarf," Cory said, but she was smiling at the idea as she stepped into the store and asked to try the suit on.

True to Annie's prediction, the off-white wool brought out all the beauty of Cory's coloring. Her blue-green eyes seemed a little deeper, more enticing, and her complexion even creamier.

"It's perfect," Annie pronounced, and Cory had to agree.

"It just needs a pale blue or green blouse to go with it," she mused, and somehow she wasn't surprised when the saleslady announced that they'd just gotten a whole shipment of new silk blouses. Cory went to the rack and immediately pulled out a pale eggshell-blue one, certain that the shade matched the swirl of blue in the scarf Buck had given her.

"I'm still not sure I can afford it," she told Annie, as the saleslady wrapped up the suit and blouse, "but clearly, somebody meant me to have that suit."

"Now, that's a more positive attitude," Annie said, patting her friend on the shoulder. "Anyway, buying new clothes is good for you."

"It is?"

"Sure. Retail therapy."

Cory was laughing as they left the store, and she was looking forward to her trip to New York more than she'd ever thought possible.

Her optimism carried her through the next couple of weeks, although she missed Buck badly, and his frequent phone calls were no substitute for the warmth of his presence.

"If I wasn't so busy, I'd drive up to Keene right now to see you," he grumbled late one evening on the phone. "I can't believe I haven't kissed you for almost three weeks."

"It's just over two," she teased him, although it felt longer to her, too. "Anyway, I'll see you this weekend."

"I know." There was a slight growl in his voice. "And not a moment too soon. What restaurant are we going to on Friday night, when you get here?"

"I thought there was a reception on Friday."

"There is, but I've already told Theodore that you and I have to leave early. He seems to think I'm responsible for getting you to do the show at all, so he's very graciously letting me have my way."

"In that case, I'd better start thinking about restaurants, I guess. It's been a while."

"It's been too long a while," he said pointedly, "for a lot of things."

And most of them, Cory knew, had nothing to do with food.

Her buoyant mood lasted right through the week and saw her through the early-morning drive to the train station in Springfield, Massachusetts. Once she was actually on the train, though, some of the nervousness she'd had about this whole project at the beginning began to bother her again.

Was this really a smart thing to be doing? Things could very easily fall apart again, leaving her lonelier and more hurt than before. It was entirely possible that she'd find Buck utterly consumed by his new business and as unwilling to compromise on that as he'd once been over his NHL career. He'd progressed far enough to admit that he tended to be obsessive about the things he wanted badly, but was he willing to change that trait in himself?

The question of the upcoming lawsuit, too, refused to go away. With Buck around, his infectious optimism had made her forget her dark forebodings for a while, but now, watching the Connecticut scenery outside the train window, she couldn't help picturing what her life might be in a year's time if the Supreme Court decided against her. Heavily in debt, with an official vote of no confidence hanging over her—there was little hope of starting a new restaurant career in *that* scenario.

Resolutely, she made herself think of other things for the rest of the four-hour trip, but when she reached New York and took a cab to the hotel where the *Five by Ten* participants were staying, a lot of the bloom had been rubbed off her excitement about this weekend.

She'd come to New York often in her Horn of Plenty days, using the trips to keep in touch with friends in the trade and to search out new ideas for her own restaurant. But since the poisonings, she hadn't ventured to the big city, and it was almost a shock now to recall the immensity of New York, and the endless streams of cars and people.

The cab pulled up in front of a new and very glossy hotel on Lexington Avenue. Inside, on the twelfth floor, she knew the reception would already be in full swing; the train schedule had forced her to be slightly late. As she waited for the elevator in the glass-and-marble lobby, her stomach fluttered nervously at the thought of seeing Buck again, of her own future, of being here at all.

Once she'd reached the twelfth floor, she forced herself to take a couple of deep breaths, and to assume the calm and elegant persona she'd cultivated when she'd been a restaurateur. The deep breathing helped, at least until she caught sight of Buck.

She saw him almost immediately, although the big room was full of people. He was talking to a couple at the other end of the room, and looking handsomer than ever in a navy suit and dazzlingly white shirt. As though she'd been sending him a signal, he turned his head when she entered, and their eyes met.

Cory could almost feel their exchange of looks. That same potent hunger was still radiating from his piercing dark eyes, and for an instant she felt his warm breath at her ear, and his hands lovingly caressing every curve and hollow of her body.

Then he glanced away, and when he looked back, his face was different, as though he'd dropped a mask over that open desire, and something had made him decide on politeness rather than passion. It only took Cory a moment to figure out why: the reception was being filmed for the TV show, and two men with minicameras were not far from Buck's shoulder, no doubt ready to record their reunion.

Well, she wasn't going to let that throw her. Threading her way through the crowd, she moved toward Buck, and held out her hand. "Hello, Buck," she said. "Good to see you again."

His skin was so warm against hers. And from the pressure of his fingers when they shook hands, she knew he was thinking the same thing she was: that if they could just get away from the television cameras, they could turn their polite handshake into the embrace they were both longing for.

They couldn't, not yet. "It's been too long," Buck was agreeing heartily, and Cory wondered if either of them had the willpower to end their handshake before it became obvious that this was far more than just two friends meeting again after a ten-year absence.

Fortunately a voice calling her name interrupted just then, and Cory turned to see Arlene, the ex-dancer who now lived in Texas. She'd even picked up a Texas accent, Cory noted, as the two women hugged and chatted over old times.

After that, it was fairly easy to keep her strong feelings for Buck hidden for the rest of the reception. She was a little cool about meeting Theodore again, although the director apologized handsomely for his underhanded maneuver in Keene.

"*Five by Ten* is just too good a project to let it go down the drain," he told her, one arm around her shoulder. "You drove me to desperate measures, my dear. But it's all right now, since you're here. Have you seen Richard yet? And Dennis is around somewhere, being unsociable."

"Dennis? Unsociable?" Cory remembered that the bespectacled archaeologist had always been friendly, if not overly talkative.

"He's discovered one of the cameramen worked on filming a dig in Iran, and the two of them are off in a corner discussing ruins. Come on, let's go get them both back on the job."

Cory had skipped lunch, and it was early evening before she got around to visiting the buffet table in the reception room. Now that her nervousness had abated somewhat, she realized she was hungry. She took a plate from one end of the table and was filling it, automatically wondering whether the Fontina cheese in the stuffed cherry tomatoes was Danish or Italian, when she heard Buck's voice at her ear.

She hadn't had a chance yet to speak to him alone, and his sudden closeness made her pulse start to speed up.

"I *think* they're looking the other way," he said.

"Who are?"

"Those damn cameras. Now I know what the lion at the zoo feels like."

Cory took a quick look around them, and saw that all the cameras were pointed in other directions. "I know what you mean," she said. He was very close to her, and she could feel the little jolt that happened every time they made contact. Even the casual touch of his hand on her shoulder had the power to conjure up a whole new world of possibilities.

"I hope you're not ruining your appetite." He nodded down at her plate.

"Not me. I just realized that two glasses of champagne on an empty stomach were making me more light-headed than they should."

"Well, don't forget our date for tonight. Have you decided where we're going yet?"

"Yes. One of my old teachers from the cooking school is running a new place in the Village. I've been dying to try it."

"Sounds good to me. Do we need reservations?"

"I already made them." She smiled at him. "I called him last night, just to chat. We have reservations for eight-thirty. I hope you don't mind my making the decision for us."

"In my experience, you're a safe person to trust when it comes to eating." He smiled back, and then added, soberly, "And if it means you're feeling excited about the restaurant business again, you know I'm all for it, Cory."

She nodded slowly, feeling her earlier excitement slowly filling her again. It was impossible to stay neutral when Buck Daly was around, she thought. And impossible not to think of making love, when his dark eyes looked so appreciatively over the trim lines of her new wool suit and the way the scarf he'd given her enhanced her coloring.

"Eight-thirty, then," he said, and she could see him struggling to rearrange his features into something more appropriate for a social gathering. Cory smiled again, and hoped the cameras didn't get too close; there was an unmistakable hunger still lingering in his eyes, and she suspected her own face looked much the same way.

By eight o'clock, the plateful of hors d'oeuvres had worn off, and Cory was feeling a hunger of a purely conventional kind. The four out-of-town participants in the show all had rooms in the hotel, and she visited hers briefly to freshen up and change from her ivory suit into a one-piece navy jumpsuit of a loose rayon material. Then she returned to the reception room to tell Buck she was more than ready for dinner.

Buck felt himself warming inside as he looked at her. The jumpsuit outlined her slim figure with a feminine allure that he found even more attractive than the formal lines of the suit, and he was glad to see she was still wearing his scarf, looped around her neck and tied under the low-cut opening of the jumpsuit's collar.

There were so many things he wanted to tell her tonight, he thought: his news about Sportsfix, mostly, but also his firm conviction that whatever happened, he didn't ever want to have to spend this long away from her again. He felt all the unspoken words building up inside him, but for the moment, he kept their conversation neutral. There would be enough time for serious talking later.

"I hope this isn't a goat-cheese pizza kind of place," he said, as they took a cab to Greenwich Village.

"Classical French, actually," she told him. "But if I know Mac—Ian MacGill, the owner—it'll be a little out of the ordinary."

That was putting it mildly, Buck thought. L'Aubergine was a small and seemingly casual place, decorated in deep greens and purples on a tan background, but he could see past the understated décor to the fact that the restaurant was very special.

The food confirmed his first impression. He was still marveling at the taste of his pepper-smoked salmon in puffed pastry when Mac himself came out to greet them and to insist that they let him open a bottle of something special to celebrate Cory's return. He was a gregarious man with an easy charm, and Cory was obviously very fond of him. She was blossoming into her old self again, Buck thought, watching her tease her former teacher and pick his brains about the New York restaurant scene all at the same time.

Mac left them alone to enjoy their entrées, but returned along with a dessert tray of some of the most incredible concoctions Buck had ever seen. "I'll never look at a Twinkie again," he muttered, choosing a slice of double-chocolate banana cake a full six inches high.

"I should hope not," Cory laughed. "Who have you got whipping up these things, Mac?"

The pastry cook had left for the day, it turned out, but Mac insisted on bringing out his chef, a classmate of Cory. "Life would be just about perfect around here," the owner muttered, "if only Ted didn't have this bee in his bonnet about going to California."

Ted was a personable man, the same age as Buck and Cory, and he staunchly defended his upcoming move. "I can't take another winter of slush," he said. "I need sunshine."

"I'll buy you a sunlamp," Mac offered plaintively, and they all laughed. "A great big one, if that's what you want."

"Sorry, Mac. Another month, and I'm gone."

When the laughter died down, Buck sensed a subtle change in Cory. He was holding her hand, enjoying the new confidence he felt in her. Now, though, he felt a tension in her slender fingers, as though she was readying herself for something.

"So who's replacing Ted, Mac?" she asked casually.

"What a good question." Mac made a face. "So far, I haven't found just the right person."

"And what qualifications does the right person need?"

Buck held his breath, as he heard a businesslike note in Cory's voice. Was she really thinking about this job? That kind of a move could solve so many of their problems.

"The right training, for one thing. A solid background in French technique. And a flair for innovation. I don't want someone who'll just imitate the bigger places."

"You interested in the job, Cory?" It was Ted, the chef, who voiced what all of them were thinking. Cory smiled, trying to seem casual.

"I might be," she said. "I've been thinking lately about getting back to work."

"I though you preferred a quieter pace," Mac said. Suddenly his outgoing charm was a little strained. "Isn't that why you went to Keene?"

"Partly. Mostly it was because my backer was there, and he would only fund a local restaurant. But I've always had a hankering to come back to New York."

"It's a crazy place to live these days," Mac told her.

"It always was," Cory replied. "Ted's leaving in a month, you said?"

"Well, by the end of March."

There were a lot of things not being said here, Buck thought impatiently. Ian MacGill clearly knew about the demise of Cory's restaurant. The question was, would he allow that to interfere with his fondness for his former student and his obvious regard for her talents?

It was hard for Buck to sit silently and listen to them negotiate in this roundabout way. He wanted to jump in and

make a statement, the way he'd done last month with
Theodore and Heck James. But this was Cory's battle, and
he forced himself to let her fight it alone.

She seemed to have decided on an open-ended offer,
something that would let Mac back out gracefully if he
wanted to. "I've been thinking about leaving the job I'm in
now," she said. "Maybe we could work a deal, Mac. I'll fill
in for Ted after he leaves—temporarily, I mean—and that'll
give me a chance to look around and assess the New York
scene for myself before I make any big decisions."

Buck couldn't help squeezing her hand in encourage-
ment. It was good to see her taking charge of her life again,
and looking beyond the negative side of what had happened to her. Maybe it was the good food and excellent
wine that had done it, or simply the excitement of being
back in New York. But for whatever reason, he felt she was
like her twenty-year-old self again, full of promise and
hope. He could see it in the shine of her blue-green eyes.

And then, as Mac answered, he saw the light in those eyes
go out, quenched by what she heard. "I'm not sure that
would work, Cory," Mac said slowly. "I'd prefer not to do
things on an interim basis. I'll do the cooking myself, if
need be, until I find someone permanent."

"I see. Well, it was just an idea."

"I have a couple of people already under consider-
ation," Mac was going on, as if trying to repair the dam-
age he saw in her face. "They look pretty promising."

"I understand. There are always lots of good people
around in New York."

Buck couldn't tell exactly what she was feeling. Bitterness? Shame at having her offer turned down? Regret at
having attempted it? One thing was abundantly clear: the
fun had gone out of the evening for her, and she was making time-to-go noises.

He couldn't stand the hidden hurt in those aqua eyes of hers. "You must be pretty tired," he said, wanting to do something to help. "You said you had to get up at the crack of dawn to catch the train."

"I did," she said gratefully. "I should get back to the hotel and get some rest. We have to work tomorrow, after all."

Mac and Ted asked some polite questions about the show, and the evening ended on a cordial if slightly strained note. Buck motioned to their waiter as Cory gathered her jacket and purse.

"The bill's been taken care of, sir," the waiter murmured in Buck's ear.

Cory overheard him. "That's very kind of you, Mac," she said, "but you didn't need to—"

"Oh, it's my pleasure." He didn't sound as though he was getting any pleasure out of it, though, Buck thought. "It's been good to see you again, Cory. Come back and visit us next time you're in the city."

Once again Buck had to bite his tongue to keep from saying something. If it had been his career that had been tainted as Cory's was, Buck knew he would probably stand up in the middle of the restaurant now and say loudly and clearly that he'd never poisoned anyone in his life, and anyone who believed he had was no friend of his. It was a physical struggle for him now, not to say the same thing on Cory's behalf.

But he knew she didn't operate that way, and he also knew she wouldn't thank him for interfering. He'd learned that much, at least.

What he *hadn't* learned was what to do next. When he'd pushed her about her career, she'd always made it clear he was doing the wrong thing. Yet to see her hurt this way wrung his heart. He settled for pulling her into his arms, once they'd climbed into a cab, and saying, "I'm sorry that had to happen."

To his surprise, she willingly let herself be drawn against his chest. "Me, too," she said. "Maybe you really *can't* go home again."

He looked down at her, and was further surprised to see a glimmer of a smile on her lips. She was more of a mystery to him than ever, and he was about to demand some explanations when the cabbie tapped on the partition and said, "Where to?"

"I was going to say the hotel," Buck said to Cory, pulling her a little closer. "But now I'm wondering if you'd rather come back to my place instead. I have these etchings, see..."

Her smile widened, and he gave his own address to the driver.

Buck's apartment looked as though a small and mostly friendly army had overrun it, Cory thought, as she stepped in the door. The place was on West 95th Street, on the fourth floor of an apartment building. It was small, comfortably furnished, and at the moment, crowded to capacity with paperwork, advertising mock-ups, blueprints, and a thousand other things pertaining to the Sportsfix clinics. Catching her eye as she entered the living room was a full-size cardboard poster of Buck himself, obviously a promotional for the new clinics.

"Sorry about the clutter." He moved some things aside, making room on the sofa for them to sit. "Our pilot clinic is just about to open, and I've been swamped with details."

"Where is it?" Cory asked.

"Chicago. Speaking of 'home town boy makes good...'" He let the words trail off, and Cory wondered if he was shying away from the reference to her own restaurant in Keene.

After a moment's silence, she turned from the cardboard cutout of Buck to the man himself, and said, "What did you think of L'Aubergine?"

"The food was spectacular. And the wine..." He moved to the shelf where he kept his bar supplies. "Speaking of which, I'm embarrassed even to look at my own stock after that, but can I offer you something to drink?"

"No, thanks." She moved to the sofa and sat down, the fabric of her blue jumpsuit draping itself over her limbs. She was silent again, and Buck couldn't help asking, "Were you serious about applying for a job at L'Aubergine?"

She leaned back against the cushions, considering his words. "I was serious about seeing what Mac's reaction would be," she said.

"What do you mean?"

"Well, anyone who knows me—and a lot who don't—are aware of the poisonings at Horn of Plenty. I just wanted to see how that would affect my reputation among old friends here in New York."

"I hate to say it, but it looks like you were absolutely right when you said the poisoning would keep you from getting another restaurant job."

Her mouth twisted into a bitter smile. "It sure looks that way, doesn't it? And if even Mac won't consider hiring me—"

She didn't finish the sentence, but looked out the window as if struck by a new thought.

"Maybe he really did have some other people lined up for the job," Buck said, playing devil's advocate.

She shook her head. "That was just a ploy," she said with certainty. "I know Mac pretty well, and I'm sure he was just looking for a way to put me off. Well, at least it was polite."

Buck still couldn't be quite sure what she was feeling. She had every right to be bitter, he thought, but there was something else in her face that he couldn't read. She seemed to be thinking hard.

Her next words were the last thing in the world he expected. "How did you manage the funding for Sportsfix?" she asked, without preamble.

"The funding for Sportsfix?" he repeated. "I thought we were talking about you."

She smiled, that enigmatic cat's smile that always drove him crazy. "Not anymore, we're not," she said. "I was just wondering who your backers were, and how you found them."

And then, instead of taking her in his arms and comforting her as he'd planned to do, he found himself hauling out financial reports and projected revenue charts, and explaining to Cory all the things she'd insisted she didn't want to hear about for the past month.

"I don't get it," he said finally, when she seemed to have asked all her questions. "I thought this was the last thing you'd be interested in."

Again she gave him that maddening smile. "I have my reasons for asking," she said. "But I don't want to go into them just yet."

"That's good." He put down the pages they'd been studying, and pulled her to him. "Because I was thinking of going into something quite different...like, for instance, the bedroom."

Her smile softened, and she put her arms around his neck. "That sounds good to me," she murmured.

There were so many things he wanted to ask her, to tell her. But they seemed unimportant compared to the feeling of holding her close to him like this and breathing in the sweet perfume of her skin. He'd spent so much time thinking of their situation together, and wondering if they could ever work out the problems that stood between them. And now, when things seemed to be coming to a head, all he could think of was the need to feel his fingers in her thick, satiny hair.

She'd twisted it up into an elegant knot behind her head today, held in place with two silver clasps. Not letting her move away from him, Buck reached one hand up and undid the fastenings, and Cory shook her head from side to side, freeing her hair in a dark blond cascade. *Honey,* he thought, drinking deep of the scent. Definitely honey. But somewhere in there, there were violets, too.

"I can never get enough of you," he said disjointedly. "Never."

He said the word with more force than he'd intended, maybe because Cory's unexplained calmness about Mac's rejection earlier this evening had made him afraid she was taking the incident as a final defeat. If that happened . . . Buck pulled her closer yet, as if trying to convince her with his strength that they had to find some way to stay together.

For the moment, at least, she was showing no signs of running away. She sighed gently at his touch, and moved against him so that he could feel the silky smoothness of her body beneath the dark blue jumpsuit. His pent-up longing for her exploded inside him at the first taste of her lips, and even the vivid dreams he'd had for the past two weeks seemed suddenly pale, mere shadows compared to the brilliance of what he was feeling now.

As they walked into the bedroom, still close together, only the very back of Buck's consciousness was giving any thought to the worries that had gone hand in hand with his passionate daydreams about Cory.

We love each other, that tiny voice told him naggingly, *but has anything really changed?*

Ten

The *Five by Ten* taping was scheduled to start early on Saturday, and Buck was the first one in line to be interviewed. "I'd forgotten what a long time it takes to put together a one-hour show," he grumbled, as his alarm clock went off beside the bed at seven. "And here I was dreaming about having some time to spend with you."

"I know what you mean." Cory moved a little closer to him under the sheet, and felt one strong arm encircling her waist after he'd finished turning off the clock radio. Her whole body felt good, and the memory of last night's passion was still throbbing pleasantly somewhere deep inside her.

She knew, though, that Buck had to be ready for the cameras at eight-thirty. *And I have things to do, too,* she reminded herself, thinking of the wakeful hour she'd spent early this morning, coming to a decision about what she should do next.

"How did you manage to be the lucky one to go first?" she asked him, as they moved apart reluctantly, stretching their limbs.

Buck swung his legs over the side of the bed. "I think Theodore figured you out-of-town types were on vacation and would want the chance to sleep in," he said, giving her a flash of his boyish grin. "I guess you were out of luck on that score, when you came home with me."

She smiled back at him. "But then, I was pretty lucky on some other scores," she assured him.

"Well, that's good to hear." He cleared his throat, and went on. "Also, I told Theodore I had to spend this afternoon meeting with some people who are flying in to apply for jobs with Sportsfix." He seemed almost embarrassed to talk about his all-absorbing project, Cory noticed.

"That's all right," she said. "I guess I'll be busy being interviewed for a good part of the afternoon, so I'll see you later at the dinner they're staging for us. And I have things of my own to do this morning, anyway."

"Visiting friends?" Buck asked.

She gave him a noncommittal smile. "Sort of," was all she would say.

They shared a cab to the hotel on Lexington Avenue, where Buck went straight to the room Theodore had set up as a studio, and Cory headed for the room she'd barely visited yesterday. She showered and changed into her ivory wool suit, and then sat down at the round table by the bed to make some phone calls.

She'd forgotten how busy a person could instantly become in New York City. Or maybe it was just the feeling of being busy, because she was surrounded by people all rushing madly on their way to somewhere. For whatever reason, by the time she'd talked to several people on the phone, arranged a breakfast meeting for the next morning, and had a quick get-together with one old colleague at eleven and a lunch date with another at noon, she felt she'd accomplished more than she ever had in a month in Keene.

"Go easy on me, Theodore," she laughed, when she breezed in to the studio room at two. "I feel like I've already done a day's work."

"And it suits you, too." The director cast an appraising eye over her. "Might I ask what you've been up to?"

"No, you might not." Cory had learned her lesson about giving too many secrets away to Theodore Aiken. "But you'll find out tomorrow, when you tape the last part of the show."

As they were seating themselves under the glare of the television lights, Theodore asked casually, "Interesting news about Buck's clinics, isn't it?"

Cory frowned. "What news is that?" she asked, not wanting to seem too interested.

"Oh, hasn't he told you? Well, I'm sure he will." The director pulled his chair a little closer to Cory's. "How's that for distance?" he called to the cameraman, and Cory was left wondering what Buck's news was, and why he hadn't mentioned it to her. Did it have something to do with his flurry of activity in interviewing people today? Maybe he'd managed to attract another big-name doctor or sports celebrity to his clinics. In her sudden change of mind about her own career, she hadn't forgotten the fact that she and Buck had never resolved this particular problem in their relationship; in fact, if her newly admitted hopes came to anything, Buck's demanding new business would be even more of an obstacle.

The thought cast a bit of a pall on her mood as she and Theodore started to chat for the cameras' benefit, discussing in chronological order what had happened to her in the

past ten years. Going into the details of the poisoning episode and her subsequent closing of Horn of Plenty, Cory
felt herself in danger of sinking into defeat again, and when
Theodore asked her about the upcoming lawsuit, it was all
she could do to keep a calm expression on her face.

Then she remembered the lessons she'd learned from
Buck's never-say-die approach to life, and the conclusions
she'd come to herself at 3:00 a.m. that morning. She sat up
a little straighter, and said, "There's a chance I could lose,
of course. But the main point is that *I* know I didn't poison anyone, and that's what I have to keep in mind when
I'm looking ahead to the future."

Theodore looked a little surprised at that, she noticed.
And well he might, when she'd insisted so adamantly that
the future was the last thing she was looking forward to just
at the moment. The director stuck to his notes, though,
obviously resisting the temptation to ask Cory what she
meant.

"We'll be interested to hear what the future holds for you
when we do the taping tomorrow," he was saying, looking
closely at her. "For now, though, I'm curious to hear your
impressions of New York, ten years after you moved away
from the city."

Cory was glad to move onto a more neutral topic. She
wasn't sure yet herself what she was going to say tomorrow, and she needed more time to think.

She didn't get much time during what was left of Saturday. Arlene insisted that they go shopping together— "I
love small-town living, but you can't get clothes like this at
home," she said excitedly, trying on a new dress in a shop
not far from the hotel—and by the time they got back to the
hotel, it was time to get ready for the gala dinner that the
television studio was hosting for the five participants on
Five by Ten.

Cory hadn't seen Buck since she'd said goodbye to him in the hotel lobby early that morning. Now, dressing for the dinner in a black crepe skirt and lustrous gold blouse that she kept for special occasions, she found herself reverting to all her earlier fears about Buck. She'd let herself fall completely under his spell again, and where was he? Off meeting with prospective employees, and letting himself be utterly absorbed in Sportsfix the way he'd been absorbed in his hockey career ten years ago.

And what about you? she asked herself. In all fairness, she had to wonder about the wisdom of the things she'd started to set in motion today. Aside from the financial riskiness of what she was proposing, she wasn't sure of her own ability to juggle a business and a relationship at the same time. It was something she'd never learned how to do, and neither had Buck. And it was possible that at the ripe old age of thirty, they were both too old to be learning this particular new trick.

She felt a lot older than that as she contemplated her uncertain future, but after a couple of minutes of staring into the mirror, she decided that worrying about it this way wasn't going to help. She'd better be concentrating on her half-finished makeup, and her hair.

The heavy satin of the full-sleeved blouse was like liquid gold when she finally stood and surveyed herself in the mirror. Her hair was swept upward, giving an elegant air to her face. She'd accented the blouse with dangling black and gold earrings, and as she stepped into a pair of low-heeled black shoes, she felt calm and poised enough to handle anything.

Except, perhaps, the sight of Buck Daly in a tuxedo. He was waiting for her outside the dining room, and as he offered her his arm, she thought all over again how attractive she found his way of moving. He had a mature athlete's confident grace, with the barely repressed exuberance of a big dog. His smile, when he looked down at her, made her want him more than ever.

"You look very dashing tonight," she commented, taking in the way the tux jacket fit his broad shoulders and tapered to his waist and hips.

"Well, I've had lots of tux practise," he said.

"You have?"

"Sure. Awards banquets, benefits and testimonial dinners. I never had an escort who looked as lovely as you do, though."

For the moment, his words were enough to make all the pains she'd taken in dressing worthwhile, and to drive away the doubts she'd felt while sitting at her mirror.

The dinner turned out to be more fun than she'd expected. The food was provided by a well-known Japanese restaurant, and Cory found herself called on to act as a guide to the various courses.

"It's all right, Richard," she said, as the actor at the head of the table looked suspiciously at his appetizers. "It's sushi."

"That means raw fish," Arlene translated.

Richard looked dubiously at them, and poked his plate with a chopstick. "Raw I can deal with," he said, "but it is *dead*, isn't it?"

"Be brave," she encouraged him. "It won't kill you."

She caught Buck's quick glance swiveling toward her, but she didn't meet his eye. Let him wonder what her unusually lighthearted reference had meant; he'd find out tomorrow afternoon.

They were still sitting at the table at midnight, reminiscing and telling stories—or rather, listening to Richard's anecdotes about life as an aspiring actor in California. It

was Theodore who finally broke up the party, comment-
ing that they hadn't been this rambunctious as teenagers.

"Just trying to recapture our lost youth, Theodore,"
Richard told him.

"Well, see that you can recapture it by eleven tomorrow
morning," the director said, rising from his chair. "That's
when the cameras start rolling, and we'll be taping all of
you together, talking about the next ten years. I don't want
you all looking so tired that the viewers wonder if you're
going to make it through ten more years!"

They took the hint, and the party dispersed. Buck hesitated at the door out into the hallway, and Cory turned to
him with a smile on her face. "I think I should repay hos-
pitality, don't you?" she asked him. "There's a nice big
double bed in my room I haven't even tried out yet."

"Seems like it would be a waste of a double bed to have
only one person in it, doesn't it?" he asked, taking her arm
again.

"That's what I was thinking."

As they waited for the elevator, Cory couldn't help saying, "Theodore tells me you have news about Sportsfix,
Buck."

"Theodore seems to be a little too free with other people's news," he muttered, and she thought he sounded angry about it.

"I just wondered if it had to do with the people you were
interviewing today," she persisted. If he was working on
signing up some celebrity for his clinics, why was he being
so secretive with her? It wasn't as though she was going to
pass the news on.

"In a way," he replied shortly. Cory was disappointed at
his abruptness, and he seemed to notice it. "I wish Theodore hadn't said anything," he added, as they stepped into
the elevator. "I'll tell you soon, Cory, I promise." His dark

eyes gleamed in the subdued lighting of the panelled elevator. "And," he added, "I think it's something you'll be
interested to hear."

More question marks, she thought, frowning at him. But
he'd clearly said all he was going to, and anyway, the way
he pulled her to him was driving out all other consider-
ations for the moment. She'd been busy all day, but the
thought of making love with Buck had never really left her
mind.

"Well," she said, taking her room key out of her pocketbook, "it sounds as though tomorrow could be a pretty
interesting day."

It had certainly started out that way, Buck thought when
he woke the next morning. They hadn't gone to sleep until
nearly two, and he was looking forward to sleeping late and
then spending most of the morning in bed with Cory, to
make up for having to get such an early start yesterday.
True, he did have to make one phone call, but that wouldn't
take long.

It was disappointing, then, to see her making motions to
get out of bed at eight-thirty.

"We don't have to be at the taping until eleven," he reminded her, as she wrapped herself in a navy bathrobe.

"I know," she said. "But I have to meet someone at
nine-thirty, and I want to have a shower and wash my hair
first. I'm sorry, Buck. I meant to tell you last night, but
somehow, I got distracted."

"Hmm." He made a move to distract her in much the
same way again, but after a moment of allowing herself to
recline against him, she moved away again, into the bath-
room.

When she came out half an hour later, dressed in her
eggshell-blue blouse and black trousers, and with her hair

dried and shining, he was lying on his back with his arms behind his head, frowning at her. "Not running around on me behind my back, are you?" he asked.

"After a night like last night?" Her slight smile drove him to distraction, and impulsively he threw back the covers and strode across the room to where she stood.

"Well, I wondered." He put his arms around her, aware of the contrast between his unclothed body and her elegantly clad one. It only heightened the primitive hunger he felt for her. "Are you sure this isn't an engagement I could talk you out of?" he growled. Her hair smelled of that eternal springtime he could always imagine when he was with her.

Regretfully, she shook her head. "You could probably talk me out of attending my own funeral, if you put your mind to it," she said, running a hand over his broad, muscled back. "But believe me, this is important to me—and to us as well, if things work out." She drew back slightly, and looked at him with an expression he couldn't quite make out. "What would you think about my moving back to New York?" she asked him, as if she was asking casually what the weather was doing outside.

"Are you kidding?" His tightened grip told her the answer. "Are you really considering it, Cory?"

"I'm considering it." Her voice told him no more about it. "And that's why I have to go and meet this person for breakfast. I'll see you at the taping, okay?"

And for now, he had to be content with that.

He'd hoped to have a quick private word with Cory before the taping started, but by the time he'd run home, showered and changed, made his one phone call and gotten back to the hotel, it was already eleven, and Cory was seated, along with the other three subjects of *Five by Ten*, at a long table which was set for lunch.

Buck made his way across the room just as the bright lights were being turned on. "Whew," he said, taking his place across the table from Cory. "I'd forgotten how hot these lights can be."

"Too bad they weren't filming last night's dinner," Richard said. "The heat might have cooked the raw fish for us."

"Oh, give us a break," Arlene kidded him. "I saw you and Dennis looking up sushi places in the phone book today in the lobby."

Richard held up his hands. "Caught in the act," he said. "I love sushi. But you know I also can't resist a good line."

Theodore appeared at the head of the table, clapping his hands to get their attention. "I'm sure you all remember how this works, even though you're thirty and starting to get senile," he said. "We'll film you during lunch—"

"I always did hate being filmed while I had my mouth full," Arlene confessed to Cory, who was next to her.

"And afterward, you'll all have a chance to tell us what your plans are for the future. In the old days we were only talking about one year at a time, but now you can look as far ahead as you want."

Buck saw Cory give a smile that only seemed half-amused. What *was* she looking forward to today? He wished he'd had a chance to tell her his good news about Sportsfix, but the problem was, he didn't want to start into the subject without going all the way and asking her to marry him and share his new life. For now, he'd have to stick with purely public revelations, and seize his chance for a private talk as soon as he could before Cory got back on the train later tonight.

When he tried to remember it later, Buck had absolutely no recollection of what they ate for lunch that day. He was barely aware of the television cameras, either. All his attention was focused on Cory, looking serenely beautiful across the table from him. For far more than ten years now, she'd been in the back of his mind most of the time; now she was the center of his whole world, and he had to know if she felt the same way about him.

Finally, when the plates were cleared, they started on the final part of the *Five by Ten* taping. Dennis went first, talking about his plans for an archaeological dig in Mexico, and about his soon-to-be-published book. Arlene spoke of her three children, and Richard gave a semi-serious account of his dual career as actor and real estate agent. Then the cameras shifted to Buck.

"I've already mentioned my sports medicine clinics," he said slowly, refusing to look into the glaring eye of the camera, but instead keeping his gaze fixed on Cory's blue-green eyes. "And I've probably given the impression that I was going to be working on those full-time for the next few years—or more than full-time. Well, they're definitely going to occupy my attention, but just today I've made a big change in the structure of the organization."

He cleared his throat and went on. "I guess I have a tendency to get a little obsessive about things," he said, and saw a couple of the others at the table smile in confirmation. "All right, then, *very* obsessive. But I'm changing that. Starting today, I'm just the figurehead for the Sportsfix complex, and I've hired a general manager who's going to have the thankless job of taking care of all the thousands of details I've been trying to cope with myself."

He looked hard at Cory now, despite Theodore's promptings for him to face the camera. "A wise person has pointed out to me that you need time in life for other things

besides your career," he concluded, "and I've finally decided to take her advice."

If he'd been looking into the camera, as Theodore was
directing him to do, he would have missed the dawning un-
derstanding on Cory's face, like a sunrise on a cloudless
morning. He saw her eyes widen, too astonished to smile
yet, and then the relentless cameraman was turning his
equipment to her, and she had to speak.

Like Buck, she held their gaze the whole time. Buck was
peripherally aware of Theodore throwing up his hands in
frustration, and motioning the other cameraman to try for
another angle. But most of Buck's attention was on what
Cory was saying.

"I've also gotten some advice from a wise person," she
said. "At least, I've had an example set for me that I'd be
foolish to miss." She looked around the table briefly, and
then back at the man across from her. "I've been really
stalled for the past couple of years, since my restaurant
closed, and I admit I've been in a panic about what will
happen if my court case goes against me. But at the same
time, I've been dying to get back into the restaurant trade,
and coming to New York again has really fired that ambi-
tion."

She took a deep breath. "So I've been looking up some
old connections of mine this weekend, and searching out
some possibilities for funding and property for a new restaurant."

"Does that mean you're thinking of coming back to New
York?" Arlene wanted to know. The camera swiveled to
catch her question.

"Yes." Cory raised her chin a little, as though daring
anyone to argue with her. "I know it's crazy, but—well,
maybe it has to do with turning thirty. You just realize that

if you don't go after your dreams pretty soon, they'll slip away on you."

Buck knew it had very little to do with turning thirty. He was clenching his fists on the linen tablecloth, fighting back the impulse to leap across the table and tell her he'd never been so proud of her. But he forced himself to sit still, and to ask a single question.

"Did something happen to change your mind, Cory?"

"A lot of things did," she admitted, smiling at him. "But perhaps the main thing was that I got turned down for a job by a man I considered an old and dear friend. And I realized then that if I was ever going to make it in the restaurant trade again, I was going to have to create my own opportunities. It's not going to be easy putting the finances together for a new place in New York, but that's not going to stop me from trying."

Her smile became self-deprecating. "It's been a while since I could think that way. But as I say, I had the example of a very pushy son of a gun in front of me, and that inspired me."

She looked over at Theodore, indicating that she was done, and before long the luncheon party broke up and the bright TV lights were turned off. Buck still felt as if there was a dazzling light somewhere, though, as he made his way over the electrical cables to where Cory stood at the other side of the table.

He'd have to take a number to talk to her at this rate, he thought. Richard was saying a fond goodbye, and getting ready to catch a cab to the airport. Dennis was telling her about someone he knew who'd backed a research grant for him once, and who might be approachable on the subject of her proposed new restaurant. Even Arlene was blocking Buck's path.

He considered bulling his way past all of them, but then he heard what Arlene had to say. "Honey, I didn't realize until I saw the clips of your interview yesterday that your poisoner was a young guy who used arsenic," she was saying, with one arm on Cory's elbow.

Cory's eyes met Buck's. Clearly, he thought, she wanted to talk to him, not to listen to any more condolences about her restaurant. "Yes," she said to Arlene. "He called himself Andy Vail."

"Vail?" Arlene's voice was an excited squeak. "Well, isn't that the strangest thing? You see, what made me ask is that my family is from Vail, and I remember my mother telling me that a couple of years ago there was a young guy who'd come home from hitchhiking all over the place, and apparently he'd tried to poison someone in his family—his father, I think it was. He was disturbed, poor guy, and they had to have him institutionalized. But it just stuck in my mind, because of the similarity with what happened to you."

By now Cory's attention was completely shifted to Arlene. "And the name Andy Vail..." she said speculatively.

"You thought it was an alias, didn't you?" Buck cut in. "Arlene, do you remember what kind of poison he used?"

"Arsenic. I remember, because it seemed like something out of a murder mystery."

"Well, you were right again, Buck," Cory said. Her eyes were as wide as Buck had ever seen them. "Looks like there may be work for your private detective, after all."

"I have his number at home," Buck said. "And we should get in touch with the police in Vail, too, and in Keene, I guess. I'll make some calls right away."

She caught at the sleeve of his suit jacket. "Not quite right away," she said. "You and I have something to talk about first."

With that in mind, it wasn't hard at all to wait while Cory finished saying goodbye to Arlene. Finally, when the two of them were alone in the hallway, he demanded, "Why didn't you tell me sooner what you were thinking of?"

"Probably the same reason you didn't tell me you were turning over the reins at Sportsfix to someone else," she returned. "I wasn't sure of all the details until just this morning, and then there wasn't time to tell you before the taping."

"Actually," he said gruffly, taking her in his arms, "the real reason I didn't tell you sooner is that I wanted to accompany the news with a proposal of marriage, and there just didn't seem to be the right time. And now I don't give a damn if the time is right or not. Will you marry me, Cory? I was as serious as I've ever been when I told you I couldn't imagine a life without you again."

"I'll marry you," she breathed, looking up at him with eyes that shone like a calm sea. "And I'll do more than that. I'll admit you've been right all along about the way I was being too cautious with my feelings."

"You had a lot to protect," he mused.

"Yes, but I've finally realized I had a lot more to lose, if I let us break up again," she said. Her smile was like a benediction now, calm and sensual at the same time.

Buck was in danger of letting ten years' worth of pent-up longing get the better of him right there in the hotel corridor when he remembered something that threw a little cold water on his exultation. He stopped kissing her long enough to ask, "What time is the train you're supposed to be on?"

"Eight," she said.

"Forget it. I can't let you go again so soon."

"I'm supposed to be at work tomorrow morning."

"Call in sick. Tell them—tell them you've got a tooth-ache. That ought to get some sympathy, from a dentist." He put an arm firmly around her shoulders and started heading toward the elevator. "Or say you pulled a muscle skating, and only an expert like me can cure you. Or tell them—" he smiled at her now, a wicked gleam in his dark brown eyes "—tell them there's a reformed jock down here in New York who desperately needs to learn how to make something besides instant coffee, and only you can teach him." The elevator door opened, but he ignored it for a long moment while he kissed her again. "Because nothing could be truer than that, Cory," he whispered, as they stepped inside the elevator together. "Only you can teach me so many things."

Epilogue

——

It was eight o'clock on a warm Friday night in June. The television was on already, but no one was watching it yet. Buck was standing on the apartment's balcony, looking down at the busy New York streets and admiring the array of vegetable plants already growing green and lush in the little balcony garden. He glanced at his watch, and then stepped in through the open door. "It's eight o'clock," he called, sitting down on the sofa.

"Coming." Cory was sitting at the dining room table, half-buried in paper—catalogs for restaurant fixtures, cookbooks, loan applications, résumés. She had the look of someone who needed to come up for air. Gratefully, she joined the man on the sofa, snuggling into the curve of his arm.

The opening credits rolled by, and Buck and Cory smiled at each other. The show was being watched by millions of viewers across the country, but no one paid closer attention than these two. The final sequence, filmed around the lunch table, seemed to interest them the most.

"I guess everybody else knew what was going on before we did," Buck said, grinning. "We barely took our eyes off each other during that whole lunch."

"At least you restrained yourself a little," Cory teased him. "Knowing you, I'm a bit surprised you didn't propose to me right there on the air."

"Would you have said yes?"

"Well, probably, but only because it would have gone so well with the kind of soufflé they were having that day. Escoffier is very specific about never combining a marriage proposal with anything except an egg dish."

Buck took a playful swipe at her, and they settled back to watch the closing credits, happy in the knowledge that the proposal referred to had been accepted and was going to be acted on next week, to be followed by an intimate dinner for friends at one of New York's most highly regarded restaurants.

As the closing credits started to roll, Cory's face became almost serious again. "Do you think there'll be another show in ten years?" she asked.

"I sure hope so. I'm looking forward to having the final taping of that one around a table in your new restaurant."

"I wish I could think of a name for it."

"How about The Fairy Princess?"

"I'll consider it."

They barely remembered to switch off the television before they moved slowly into the bedroom at the back of the

apartment. And there, as far as they were both concerned, was where they would find the happiest of all possible endings.

* * * * *

Silhouette Desire

COMING NEXT MONTH

RUN FOR THE ROSES
Peggy Moreland

Alyssa McCord would have done anything to save her family home — she even tried her luck at the races! Stuart Greyson had plans for Al's land, but could he put profit before the feelings Alyssa generated?

AFTER YOU
Helen R. Myers

A decade ago, proud heiress Elizabeth Beaumont Kirkland had narrowly resisted her reckless attraction to her father's rugged horse trainer. Now Morgan had come back to the area as a prominent landowner, but would the past always separate them?

SLOW DANCE
Jennifer Greene

Max Carlson should have known he was in trouble when he stopped to help a woman motorist and ended up delivering her baby! But when Kitt and the baby showed up at his farm he was lost. Were they going to break his heart?

Silhouette Desire

COMING NEXT MONTH

WINTER MORNING
B J James

As magnificent and powerful as a Viking god,
Zachary Steele had been Christen Laurence's friend
throughout their medical training. Then a single
night of overwhelming passion changed their lives
forever...

CAT'S PLAY
Naomi Horton

Rand Gallagher was a man who usually got what he
wanted and as soon as he saw Cat Bradshaw, he
knew he wanted her. But how could he convince her
that he wanted Cat more than her money?

THAT'S MY BABY
Judith McWilliams

Lucy Hartford decided to have a baby but there was
a mix-up and suddenly her baby had a father. How
could she fight a man who had practically moved in
and was pampering her shamelessly?